TWENTIES TALK

TWENTIES TALK

The Unpaved Road of Life After College

Michael Levy

Writers Club Press
San Jose New York Lincoln Shanghai

Twenties Talk
The Unpaved Road of Life After College

Writers Club Press
an imprint of iUniverse, Inc.

For information address:
iUniverse, Inc.
5220 S. 16th St., Suite 200
Lincoln, NE 68512
www.iuniverse.com

This is a work of fiction. All events, locations, institutions, themes, persons, characters and plot are completely fictional. Any resemblance to places or person, living or deceased, are of the invention of the author.

ISBN: 0-595-24193-X

Printed in the United States of America

For My Brother Jason

"*When I was young, I had to choose between the life of being and the life of doing. And I leapt at the latter like a trout to a fly. But each deed you do, each act, binds you to itself and its consequences, and makes you act again and yet again. Then very seldom do you come upon a space, a time like this, between act and act, when you may stop and simply be. Or wonder who, after all, you are.*"

—Ursula K. Le Guin, *The Farthest Shore*

Acknowledgements

Jason. Thanks so much for your help. No words of gratitude can even compare to the time and energy you put into this project. I can't thank you enough for the countless hours spent editing my book, while asking nothing in return. You encouraged and inspired me, and your faith in me never wandered. Your intangibles will always be recognized. I love you very much. Thanks bro.

Mom & Dad. Thanks for your eternal love and support. I'm really lucky to have two people who care so much.

Matt, Lawrence, Barry, and Jason. Thanks for always taking care of your little brother, and for being my best friends. Always.

Josh. My "Creative Consultant," your editing and support throughout the whole process was invaluable. Thanks.

Dan. Thanks for editing my book despite my nagging emails.

Finally, thanks to the family and friends who read my work before it was published. Your thoughts and encouragement gave me the strength to finish this project.

Introduction

"Experience is not what happens to a man. It is what a man does with what happens to him."

—Aldous Huxley

I still remember the crack of the bat. A screaming line drive left me a sitting duck. The ball hit me square in the face; blood gushed out and turned the mound red. I was rushed to the hospital for what turned out to be emergency surgery to repair my broken jaw. It was the nastiest accident I had ever seen in person, and worst of all, I was the victim.

I ended up getting lucky. Really lucky. I could have died if the ball was six inches higher. Perhaps that sounds over-dramatic, but it certainly felt that way. After six months of recovery, all the while working for a start-up technology company and hating my job, I knew I had to make a change. My accident completely changed my outlook on life. A shattered jaw served as my wake-up call. My priorities shifted. Corporate America wasn't making the grade, at least for now. There was nothing rewarding about being an analyst at a desk job. Work was extremely boring, and provided little satisfaction. I felt I was too young to be settling for a life that I did not want, and I knew I had lots to offer.

I didn't realize that graduating from college and starting a career would be such a big transition. I always considered college the "good life," but I didn't know how good it was until I entered the working world. I figured I would work for a couple of years after I graduated and then go back to school and get my MBA. I thought life would be a simple riddle that I could easily decipher. Instead, I quickly learned that it was more confounding than a Rubik's Cube—a puzzle that, to this day, I still cannot solve.

I was certain about one thing; I *didn't* know what I wanted to do with my life! Most people I talked to agreed that I needed to get away, to refocus and channel my newfound energy and outlook into something more rewarding than a monotonous desk job. That much was obvious. Luckily, an unexpected opportunity presented itself. All you can ever ask for in life is an opportunity. It's up to you to act on it when it comes up. And, that is just what I did.

WEDNESDAY

CHAPTER 1

"When you do the common things in life in an uncommon way, you will command the attention of the world."

—George Washington Carver

I desperately needed a beer to relax me from the stresses of my job, so I decided to head to a local bar after work to watch one of the early, meaningless college football bowl games. The game was not an exciting match-up; Purdue versus Missouri isn't exactly must see television. However, when you call your bookie and put $300 on the game, as I had just done, the match becomes a tiny bit more intriguing.

As I walked into the bar, I found it busier than I had expected. I wanted to watch the game in peace, but with the amount of people that were there, my hopes of being alone with my beer and my bet were unlikely to be fulfilled. Up at the bar were two bartenders, one that looked like an ex-football player, and the other a stunning blond with hair that came down to her shoulders. She had the body of a model. She was barely wearing any clothing, and what she was wearing didn't leave much to the imagination. Now, it's a known fact that women bartenders pull bigger tips from male customers, and it is women like this bartender that make that claim indisputable. Somehow, I managed to find my way to her side of the bar, right by the television, and grabbed a seat.

"Hey, what's going on?" I said to the blond bartender, affecting my most confident intonation.

I knew right off the bat that I had no chance with this girl. She was way out of my league. I was playing for the Durham Bulls, and she was pitching for the New York Yankees. She was probably thinking, "Here's another asshole I have to serve." She looked my way, nodded, and replied in an authoritative tone, "Hey, so what do you want to drink?"

"Sierra Nevada."

She went over to the tap and started pouring my beer. As she looked across the room and away from me, she offered me the perfect chance to look her over and stare at her amazing breasts. She knew that I was committing this filthy act. I knew that she knew, and we both knew that she would get a bigger tip because of it.

"$3.00 for the beer," she said as she handed me the pint over the bar counter. I took out my wallet and handed her a $5 bill.

"Keep it!" She gave me a half-assed nod and didn't even say the magic words, "thank you."

I gave her a good tip and she couldn't even acknowledge me. If the ex-football player was my bartender, I would have asked for a dollar back. She knew she was the reason for the extra buck. I started sipping the beer so it wouldn't spill over, all the while trying to rationalize why I gave her the extra cash. The only thing that came to mind was that staring at her and talking to her, even if it was for only a minute, was worth the extra money. Pathetic, maybe, but I was no different from any other guy. Looking back, all she was to me was a classy peepshow, and the truth of the matter is that there really isn't much difference these days (if there ever was). One dances while another serves beers. Either way, both types of women are trying to make money by exploiting men. I just wanted to watch the football game. Another woman taking advantage of a defenseless horny male.

The second half of the football game was about to get underway as I finally got comfortable at the bar. I had bet Purdue, minus one point. Purdue was losing the game 14-13, but plenty of time was left for me to win my $300.

After sitting there for about ten minutes, this sexy brunette slipped off her jacket and grabbed the empty bar stool to my left. I didn't get a great look, but I knew this girl would now be on my mind throughout the rest of the game. She was simply too attractive to ignore. As she sat down, I gave her a friendly nod, said hello, and went back to watching the game. I didn't want her to realize she already had me mesmerized. She ordered a beer from the bar. Five minutes later we finally spoke to each other.

"Yes, touchdown!" I said. Purdue scored to go up 20-14. I was winning my bet.

"Who's playing?" She replied.

"Purdue versus Missouri. Alamo Bowl."

"Did you go to Purdue?"

"No, I went to Michigan, another Big-10 school. Gotta pull for my conference." I didn't want to mention that I had $300 on the line. Not yet at least.

"Michigan. Great school. Football must be crazy there."

"I never miss a game. You'll always see me at a bar early in the morning on Saturday." I lived in San Francisco.

"Which bar do you go to watch their games? I actually went to Bayside last week with a few friends to watch some games."

"I usually go to Bayside. I also go to Kezar's or The Bus Stop. So, are you a football fan?" This is the all-important question.

"Yes and no. I'll go somewhere to watch a sporting event with my friends if it's a big game, but I definitely don't understand the intricacies of the game. I know the basics."

After years of careful research, I have ascertained that there are four types of women in this world when it comes to sports. Although it is possible for women to straddle multiple categories, these four cover the basics:

1. *The Hater*—These women hate sports and do not want to be involved at all in a sports conversation. They will never watch a game on television, not even with their boyfriend or friends. They see sports as a stupid activity that really has no importance at the end of the day. The chances of me dating one of these girls are as high as me dunking a basketball. Zero.

2. *The Watcher*—These women are totally into watching sports, but have never played a game in their life. They think they know a lot about sports, but often their assessment of games or plays is incorrect. I have a M.S.K. degree, that is a Masters in Sports Knowledge, and it bothers me when a woman who has never played a certain game thinks they know more than I do. These women can be the most frustrating of all, and therefore are undateable.

3. *The Facilitator*—These women take an interest in sports, but don't really have a vested interest in any particular team. It is an aspect of their life, but far removed from the things they care for most dearly. They will understand enough about sports to get by, but do not and never claim to know the intricacies of the sporting event at hand. These types of women will make sports a bigger part of their life if their boyfriend enjoys sports as well. If a woman in this category is truly superb, she will make snacks while you watch football games with your buddies. Most importantly, she will never interrupt you during 4th downs, goal line stands, or when there is less than two minutes left in a game or a half. Facilitators rank second highest in terms of dateability.

4. *The Enthusiast*—These women have always enjoyed playing and watching sports. They will go to sports games with you, and

actually want to go to the game. They have no problem getting into a sports conversation, and they understand your pain when your team loses a game. In fact, these women have a favorite team and hurt like men do when their team loses. They know all the "rules" that Facilitators might take some time to learn, or never will bother to figure out. This type of women is my ideal girlfriend.

By her initial comments, I had a good feeling that the girl I was talking to at the bar was somewhere among the Facilitators, maybe a tad Hater, but all together rating pretty high on my dateability scale.

"Well, at least you know your limits," I said.

"I like watching football games with my boyfriend," she remarked.

Great. Just what I needed to hear. She's throwing out the boyfriend line this early in the conversation. Am I that pathetic? Fine, I was sitting here first. Let me watch the football game in peace.

"When I have a boyfriend that is."

Back from the grave? Was that a come on? I wasn't sure. Rarely has a girl come on to me, and definitely not lately.

"What? On the couch all cuddly?"

"Yes. I love doing something with my guy that he enjoys. Of course I expect the same in return."

"Of course."

"But that never seems to happen."

"Tell me about it…I can't catch a break either."

"You, no way…you're so handsome."

Who is this girl?

"Don't take this the wrong way, but you're pretty straightforward."

"Usually, I sit at bars and guys are all over me, like there was nothing else in their lives before I arrived. You were polite, but the game was still your main focus. I liked that."

"But I was thinking about you the whole time. Do you know how difficult it is to watch a game when a beautiful women is sitting next to you?"

"No, I don't…. You think I'm beautiful?" My famous "magic" was starting to kick in.

"I have been thinking of what I should say to you for the last 10 minutes, agonizing over my pickup line. And yes, you are gorgeous. Just my type actually."

"And what type might that be?"

"Brunette. 5′5″. Nice smile. Great legs."

"And you think I'm straightforward! So, do you live around here?"

"Yeah, about a five minute walk. You?"

"About the same. I was supposed to meet a friend at the bar, but she just called me on my cell phone and told me she couldn't make it. I figured I'd grab a beer while I'm here."

"One woman's loss is another man's gain."

"You're so sweet!"

We ended up talking for the next 20-30 minutes. I was having a great time flirting with her, and more importantly, Purdue had just scored a touchdown with seven minutes left in the 4th to go up 30-28.

"So you hate your job. What are you thinking about doing?" She said.

"I'm not sure. I was thinking about teaching, but I don't have a certificate, and I have very little experience in the classroom. Most of my friends think I would be a great teacher, though. I really like the idea of doing something like teaching, which is obviously rewarding and where everyday is totally different, even if the money isn't so great…. Yes! Interception, Purdue." I had told her about my little wager.

"Well, let's see what type of teacher you would be…. Teach me football in the five minutes that are left in the game."

"Teach you football? Now? What do you want to know?"

"You're the teacher, you tell me what I need to know. Come on, educate me!"

"All right…well…I guess the first rule of teaching is to figure out how to relate your topic to something you understand."

"Okay, I'm listening."

"Since football isn't your forte', I guess the only thing I can think of that you'd be sure to relate to is sex."

"Excuse me? I would leave the classroom right now…if I didn't like you."

"Just go with me here. Okay, I know you understand first downs and touchdowns, but you probably don't understand what each player's responsibilities are, and how all the players function together as a team."

"Yeah, that's about right."

"Okay, good. Today we will go over the offense and next week on my couch we will discuss the defense."

"That depends on if I drop your class."

"That's not likely. Now, imagine that the offense is a man having sex with a woman, with each position—quarterback, running back, wide receiver, and offensive lineman—representing a body part. The key is that they all have to work together to score a touchdown, literally and figuratively."

"This sounds interesting. I might need another beer."

"Okay. What do you want? My treat." Now that I was hitting on this girl, combined with the fact that my bartender was still the beautiful blond, I would give an even bigger tip than last time. I ordered the beers, left a three-dollar tip, and continued my lecture.

"The QB is the man's penis. The QB usually places the fate of the rest of the team on his shoulders. The QB cannot get too excited—he might blow a pass or strike to early, if you know what I mean—and more than any other player he must earn his teammates' trust. If the QB has a bad game, even if all the other players do their part, well, we all know the sad end to that story."

"Did you read this in *Maxim* or some men's magazine? This is either going to be very interesting or a total waste of my time."

"Came up with it when I was sitting around drinking beers and watching football with my friends, actually."

"I'd like to be there to watch a football game with you and your friends!"

"I'm finding my rhythm here, so let's get back to my discussion of the QB. The quarterback also takes most of the blame for a loss, whether it be due to a lackluster performance, read 'couldn't get it up,' or by letting the game getting away from him and losing his composure, shall we say, a bit too early. Of course, with great risk comes great reward. If the QB has a stellar performance, he will receive great press—I don't have to tell you how women gossip—and many endorsements."

"But, I find that you can tell a lot by the way a man kisses. That's really important to me. Don't get me wrong, the quarterback is important, but kissing sets the tone."

"Funny you said that, because in football if you can't run the football, you're not going to win many games. That's why running backs are like a man's lips. Just as you said, kissing breaks down a woman's defense and opens up other areas for exploitation. The running back has to find the woman's weak spots, which may be up the middle, on the lips, or by sweeping to the sides, in search of the ears and neck. Big fullbacks like Mike Alstott usually go up the middle and are more aggressive in their kissing, while halfbacks like Warrick Dunn apply more of a finesse game that emphasizes nibbling and soft, slow kisses."

"Those guys play for Tampa Bay, right? I'm from Florida originally."

"You know your stuff! Impressive! The last thing I would say about running backs is this. When a running back breaks a big run, it's like a man using his lips down field! Huge, and almost certain to lead to a score! So, there are many ways in which the running back opens up the field and makes life easier for the quarterback and wide receivers. If you can see that this is true in the realm of sex, you're at least one step further along in your understanding of the game of football."

"I don't even want to know what the wide receivers are, do I?"

"What do you think is the most important skill for a wide receiver to have?"

"I don't know, I guess he has to be able to catch the ball."

"You got it! Wide receivers are a man's hands. Wide receivers are used to stretch out the defense and to gain big yards going for deep passes. The wide receiver needs to take advantage of the tone set by the running back by zigzagging down field. That way the wide receiver can determine how much room the opponent is going to give the offense to maneuver. The wide receiver could go for a short pass, say a hand up the shirt, or take a chance and go deep, a hand down the pants. What people may not see, in either sex or football, is that wide receivers have to figure out what type of defense their opponent is playing. If the woman is playing a soft-zone, a wide receiver should of course take what the defense is willing to give, which will be the short pass. Why fight for 20 yards when you're going to get a first down with no effort at all? Then, as the defense switches to man-to-man, long passes become more possible. Now, that the short pass has been established, the wide receivers should go deep and try to catch a bomb for a big gain!"

"This is absolutely hilarious. Very clever!"

"Thanks. I figure everything relates to sex anyway, so why shouldn't football."

"Good point. But you're missing one thing. If the guy doesn't have a personality he ain't getting into my pants."

"I couldn't agree more. Maybe you should be a football coach. Any true football fan knows that the offensive linemen win the game in the trenches. The offensive linemen set the tone for the entire offense throughout the game. That's why they are a man's mouth, or more to the point, his personality. The offensive line hardly gets noticed during sex, but everyone knows that it's the key to a successful team. All the other players are extremely grateful to the offensive line, mind you, especially the QB and running backs." I swig back the rest of my beer, and turn back to the game. "So, I guess that's football in a nutshell. What do you think?"

"Well, I think you could be a good teacher. You're funny, insightful, and nuts!"

"All right, hold on a second. Purdue is down one and is kicking a field goal for the win."

Within the confines of my own head, I commenced my pleadings and prayers to the football Gods. Like it or not, when it comes to sports, we're all pagans (And I'm Jewish!). Even if you're just a "please, please, please" sort of guy, you're pleading to some higher power, and I assure you it's not the same higher power you pray to in church, temple, or what have you.

"Well, how about if they win we leave this bar and grab a nice meal downtown? If they lose we call it a night and go home," she said.

"Sounds good."

"This is too much pressure for a new fan!" She couldn't even bare to look.

"It's good! Yes!" I stopped myself from hopping up and down and doing my little victory dance. I knew I would pay later for failing to follow through on any part of my post-game ritual, but other forces were at play and I didn't want to damage what was turning out to be an exceptional evening. "You have just earned yourself an all expense paid meal!" I said.

"Sweet! This was so much fun!"

"You ready to get out of here?" We grabbed our coats and started to head for the exit.

"Yep. Hey teach, what body part is the field goal kicker?"

"Actually, special teams players aren't body parts. They aren't absolutely necessary for your team to win, but can be extremely important to the final result."

"In other words...?"

"A field goal kicker is the condom!"

"Oh my god..."

"Just like a kicker, he sits quietly on the sidelines all game, but in the end he will make or break your night!"

We ended up grabbing a nice dinner downtown, and then she came back to my place. Like all women, she said she didn't normally do this type of thing. True or not, to her credit, it was one of the more memorable evenings of my life. And in case you're wondering, my boys came up big. My running back ran for well over a hundred yards, although that came as no surprise. He's been invited to the Pro Bowl eight years in a row. My quarterback, aided by my superior offensive line, played a flawless game and always kept the defense on its toes.

Most importantly, my field goal kicker came up big again!

THURSDAY

CHAPTER 2

"If you are going through hell, keep going."

—Sir Winston Churchill

Except for my lucky rendezvous the previous night, I hadn't been with a woman in a while. However, that was not the main cause of my misery. The reason I was miserable was that I had a job that I despised more than Ohio State (Wolverines and Buckeyes do not get along). My job was the most boring, unfulfilling thing I had done in my whole life. Let me put it this way: had I spent my entire childhood concocting the worst possible scenario for my career, it could not have been more boring and unfulfilling than what had in fact come to pass.

While people tend to get caught up in each moment and frustrated with every little momentary distraction, the reality is that only a few important events define our lives. For me, one such incident was my softball accident; for others, it may be a rejection letter or being fired from a job. What we do with our lives after these moments is of utmost importance. Many people go on as if life has not changed; that they simply encountered a small setback, and that they should not pause, but forge on with whatever they were already doing. There is nothing wrong with that strategy, but for me, stumbling on with my current life wasn't making me happy.

What type of work was I doing during my youthful twenties, the time, which, according to many, I was supposed to be enjoying the most? I guess the only way to illustrate my misery is to describe my typical day at the office. I was an analyst for a technology company, assigned to a tiny cubicle, where I stared at a computer and crunched numbers all day. Here we go—hold on for the ride:

6:50 AM My alarm goes off. I press snooze. The snooze, as we all know, is a man's best friend or his worst enemy.

6:59 AM I wake up again and get out of bed. This way I can still tell people that I wake up before seven. I run through my standard self-interrogation while I stare at my reflection in the mirror. Why didn't I get the memo about life in the corporate world? Why didn't anyone ever tell me about the "quarter-life crisis?" Why didn't anyone tell me about this thing called "work" after college? Why did they teach me philosophy and psychology, and fail to offer a class entitled something like, "Corporate America: Everything You Don't Want to Hear but Need to Know Before You Enter the Workforce"? Or was all this perfectly clear to everyone else and I just had my head in the sand?

7:15 AM I eat a "hardy" breakfast consisting of Rice Krispies Treats, while reading the college football section of the sports page. This ritual leads to inevitable reminiscing about the good old days in college when, in my junior year at Michigan we went undefeated and won the National Championship. How, at any time, I could go on a road trip and visit one of my friends at a different school. Then I start thinking about how current students have no idea about the true meaning of hard work. College students think that studying is just as tough as going to work every day. Sure, college students put in late nights and study a fair amount for exams, but that just falls between the parties and football games. In my college experience, I found the football games to be the most stressful part of college life (lose one game and the season is over), with going to classes and taking exams the easy part.

The first problem with today's work environment is that there is no longer an 8-hour day. The idea of working from 9 to 5 is no longer a possibility. It's a myth, a fantasy. A 9 to 5 job is like Kayser Soze from *The Usual Suspects*—once it's gone, it's gone forever. This doesn't even count the commute. My drive to work usually takes an hour, and I typically leave work for home around six in the evening. That means I don't walk up my front steps until around seven, if I'm lucky. By the time I read my mail, change clothing, prepare my "specialty" of macaroni & cheese and clean up, it's already eight and almost time for bed. At this point, all I want to do is sit on the couch and watch television. But, if you do that all the time, you're considered boring! You'll become nothing but your work, and let me tell you, it happens a lot faster than you think.

7:30 AM As I mentioned, the commute is a bitch. If I could work eight hours and at the end of the day walk five minutes to my apartment, maybe I would have more time to do things I like. Maybe, I could have a hobby or two. Unfortunately, my commute seems like it takes roughly the same amount of time as it does to drive across the country. When I was growing up, my parents never seemed to be so upset about their commute to work. I didn't even really think about the idea until after I graduated. Then I realized it isn't that my parents don't get just as frustrated as I do, but rather they are desensitized to the length of the commute, which over the course of their generation creeped up on them at a rate of perhaps five minutes every five years or so. In any event, they apparently have come to realize that there is nothing that can be done. For me, it was as if I was suddenly thrown into the fires of traffic hell. I suddenly lost approximately 10-20 percent of my waking hours and, at this point in my life, I don't want to concede up to three hours of each day just to get to and from work.

The problem with the commute these days is that rush hour keeps on getting longer and longer as more and more cars hit the road. Rush hour used to be from 8-9 AM and 5-6 PM. Now it's every hour of the day EXCEPT 10 AM-2 PM. Even more frustrating are the carpool lanes. As you know, if you have more than one person in the car, you're allowed to drive in the carpool lane without getting a ticket. Do you know how frustrating it is to be stationary in a traffic jam while the lane next to you is almost empty? If you do NOT develop road rage upon witnessing this spectacle day in and day out, you should seek help from a psychiatrist.

Interestingly, the government thinks these lanes help reduce the commute time and encourage carpooling. It takes me on average one hour to get to work by myself. If I pick up my friend so I can take advantage of the carpool lane, it will take an extra 10 minutes to get to his house and I would waste another 10 minutes dropping him off at his office. Meanwhile, I can save perhaps 20 minutes on the highway in the carpool lanes. In other words, it's a wash. I will have saved NO time. Worse, I now have to coordinate times with my buddy.

You know there's a problem when you see other drivers cheating the system by using inflatable dolls as a second passenger. If the government isn't going to correct the problem, well then you're going to have to find your own solution. I am of the opinion that the dolls are a creative way to trick cops into thinking you qualify to drive in the carpool lanes, and I am wholeheartedly behind people who choose that option.

Finally, what bugs me the most is seeing mothers with two kids in the carpool lane. I know for sure that their children do not have any important meetings to attend, unless you consider Barney or a soccer practice important. I honestly believe I see more mothers in the carpool lanes than any other group of drivers. [Note to mothers: If you are also working, please disregard the preceding paragraph.]

The only positive of a long commute is the opportunity to listen to the Howard Stern Radio Show. Stern is the only guy on radio that I can count on for a good laugh. When you go to work depressed, nothing is better than a little humor to brighten your day. I'm not sure why people dislike him so much. He speaks the truth, the truth in his mind at least, which is a lot more than most people can say. Yes, sometimes he is vulgar, and sometimes he is off-the-wall, but no one wants to listen to an average Joe. If they did, I would be on the radio.

All I want to do in the morning is laugh and keep my mind off the impending eight hours of hell. Stern only claims to be an entertainer. He isn't trying to save lives or preach gospel. People can just turn off the radio if they don't like him. Honestly, this is America, and the whole point of America is we have the right to choose. I choose to listen to Stern. You can listen to the news. What I like about Stern is that he succeeded through hard work, creativity, and persistence. He obviously didn't succeed because of his looks. He made it because he related to a big group of people who enjoy listening to his program. People should respect that Stern, and few others, bring smiles to people's faces every single day. Stern has a gift that most people only dream of attaining. In some weird way, he is a spiritual healer. No matter how crazy that may sound, I think you know what I'm saying.

8:45 AM After I park my car, I have to walk five minutes to the office. On my walk, I encounter bums on the street panhandling. I have no problem whatsoever with people begging on the street; my problem is that I think they can do a better job at being a bum! Bums have no clue on how, and where, to beg for money. They always seem to be in the worst spots, or show up unprepared, i.e. without a little box or cup for you to donate your money. If bums learned a few important sales techniques to improve their panhandling skills, they would be much more successful. If they would take a little more pride in being a bum, they could triple their income in one week! Maybe I could teach a class, Bum 101. The classroom could be the sidewalk, 3rd and Market, with classes MWF.

I find it interesting that so many people think that bums could get a job if they cleaned up their act a bit. I always wonder if those people would hire a bum if they were to read one of these bum's resumes. I can't see an employer hiring someone whose experience reads: Mug Holder, 1995-2001; preceded by Street Orator 1993-1995. Then, when the employer asks what is the best way to contact the applicant, he/she responds that they live nearby, in the alleyway on Market St., in a box.

8:45 AM I finally walk into the office, head over to my desk, and see the red blinking light on my phone indicating that I have voice messages. I usually try to get in about 15 minutes before nine, the time when my boss gets into work, because that way it will look like I have been working since early in the morning. I listen to my voice messages while turning on my computer. It's my boss, which cannot possibly be a good thing. He tells me that today's meeting is cancelled. Moreover, since the VP that we were going to meet with lives in a different city, it is more than likely that the meeting will never occur. I am not normally a fan of having to go to a meeting, but this meant that everything I had worked on for the past month was garbage. I was supposed to give a 15-minute presentation, and had prepared a 30-page report, which I could now put right through the shredder. Essentially, with one phone call, I was told that everything I worked on the past month was pointless and a waste of time. (Okay, I know that I am setting out of my normal work day and that this call from my boss wasn't an everyday affair, but it was extremely traumatic to my young professional psyche, and I think I'm due a little leeway for mild histrionics.)

9:00 AM The first thing I do on my computer is check my personal and work email. Since the majority of my friends are on the East Coast, that first click on "Inbox" can set the tone for the rest of the day. East Coasters get to work 3 hours before I arrive, so by the time I get to my desk I would hope that at least a couple of my friends have sent me a message. The more messages I get from friends, the less time to think about the horrible day ahead. By the time I reply to my friends and send emails to co-workers about things like who should be responsible for buying the birthday cake for a co-worker, almost an hour of my workday has passed without any actual work being done.

10:00 AM It has been almost three hours since I had my "nutritional" breakfast, and I'm starting to get hungry. I stroll down to the local coffee shop and pick up my usual bagel with butter. Sometimes I go crazy and get an Egg McMuffin at McDonald's. When McDonald's becomes "crazy," there is definitely something wrong with your life.

During my journey for food, I usually run into one of the interns picking up food for their lazy boss. Interns believe that working these jobs is fun, and that what they do is real work. They believe that a three-month internship at a big accounting or consulting corporation is the same as working a full-time job. What they do not realize is that they've only received a small fine, a misdemeanor, in the criminal court of life, while I have been convicted of a felony and sentenced to work for the rest of my living days! As an intern, you know your position will be done at the end of the summer, no matter how boring and unfulfilling it is. The internship is just a quick fix between school years. Interns are wined and dined and treated like kings for three months, and for some reason become blinded by this fantasy treatment. They never realize that this vocational oasis will quickly transform into a barren desert when they begin working full-time after graduation. I try to explain this to some of the cooler interns, but it never seems to really hit them until they sit next to me the following year and suddenly become just as miserable as me.

10:30 AM Now I am ready to get serious about my work...well, maybe not just yet. Surfing the Internet is part of the research side of my job and I usually start my "research" in the world of sports, beginning with ESPN.com. ESPN.com is my morning cup of coffee. I need it to fight off the constant yawns of boredom while I stare at my computer. My favorite time of year is during the late fall/early winter, when the selection of sporting events is a virtual cornucopia of choice. Not only are college and pro football playing the most important games on their schedule, but also college and pro basketball are just getting under way. With so much sports activity going on it's easy to understand why I spend the next 30 minutes reading articles, checking out the standings and statistics, and of course, improving my fantasy league teams.

Luckily for me, techies, while not considered the most extroverted individuals in the world, are wise to the wily ways of Corporate America. The keyboard stroke of Alt-Tab might be their greatest creation to this day, rising above even the computer itself. Alt-Tab is the best way to quickly change the open program on the screen so that when your boss walks by your desk it will look like you are hard at work on some spreadsheet on Excel.

During March Madness, it is a whole different story. March Madness is more important than work. It's only three weeks a year, and like I said before, work is forever. The pressure of pressing Alt-Tab when my boss walks by is no longer necessary. My boss can watch me enter 10 pools for the next hour and I wouldn't care one bit. During the Madness, my lunch usually starts at noon and ends at four when the final game of the afternoon session finally ends.

I know I could spend more than 30 minutes on ESPN.com, but I have to be responsible. I do have a job to do, after all. Besides, I know I will be back to the site throughout the day. Any good employee knows how to balance their schedule and manage their time. I am one of the best in making sure I fit ESPN.com into my schedule at least twice every day. Yet another reason why I am such a valued employee.

After ESPN.com, I visit Yahoo! Finance and check my stock portfolio. In the good old days, I was looking at updates every minute, thinking that the market was so good that I could make a few grand each hour. And sometimes I did. Now, with the "dot-bomb," I hardly visit the Finance section at all. It's depressing to see my portfolio balance these days. All you read about is how your stock tumbled $20 a share because the company missed earnings by three tiny little pennies. Three little pennies cost me thousands of dollars. Go figure.

11:25 AM Alt-Tab

11:30 AM I start thinking about lunch and all the fast food options I have nearby. Then I start to get depressed over the fact that I will probably end up eating with one of my unfriendly co-workers. By the time I get my belongings together, ask around to see who is going out to lunch, and wait for everyone else to get ready, it's already noon.

12:00 PM We head out to lunch somewhere nearby, but I wish it was off on another planet. I am one of those people that has to get out of the office for lunch. I just do not want to eat in front of my computer; hell, I stare at it all day. Also, my boss' office is right behind me, and I hate thinking about him or her seeing how long I take to eat my lunch. I usually eat fast food, and that's one reason I am in the worst shape of my life. Maybe it's also because I have no time to go to the gym anymore. Probably both. It usually takes me about 45 minutes to eat my lunch, but my lunch break is far from over. I always have a few errands to run, e.g. going to the bank, picking up some toiletries, buying some new clothing, or at the very least staring dumbly into space. Also, lunch lines at these places are so long that sometimes you will find signs that read, "If you are standing here, it will take at least 45 minutes to get to the front." While I am impatient about almost everything else I do in life, when it comes to lines that give me less time in the office, you will usually find me with a big smile. Come on, I am being paid to stand in line!

1:30 PM Now the day is just over half done. I know my boss likes to eat late lunches, so coincidentally I like to eat early lunches. This way I minimize the time available for my boss to breathe down my neck. I follow the same philosophy during the Christmas/New Year's period when everyone goes away on vacation. I love working that time of year because no one is there, and the employees that are there do virtually no work. Then, when it's the busy season, I always seem to be on vacation. Genius, right?

Obviously, after an "exhausting" morning and an all too short lunch, I need to go to the lounge to grab a cup of coffee. Typically, there will be a co-worker in the lounge, so we chitchat for a few minutes, and then finish off the conversation by saying the typical business world phrases. My favorites are: "Gotta run, I'm swamped," or "I'm so busy. I have three meetings to prepare for, all this afternoon." We each know that the other is full of shit, but let me tell you something; more crap comes out of the mouth of business people than out of a horse's ass.

2:00 PM The day has finally reached the heart of the afternoon, the part that I consider gut check time. It's time to get serious. But, then I remember AOL Instant Messenger (IM). I begin instant messaging my buddies since I am bored out of my mind, and I know they are as well. Two o'clock is the perfect time for everyone to use IM because I'm still getting organized after lunch and my buddies in the East are on their stretch run before leaving work. They want to talk about their plans for the night while I get to discuss why Boston Chicken is worth the extra buck over McDonald's. It's a perfect match. AOL Instant Messenger is the savior of the corporate world desk job.

2:57 PM Alt-Tab

3:00 PM At last, important work to be done. This would include paying my cable bill, dividing the telephone bill, and of course, setting doctor's appointments in the heart of upcoming work days. Three o'clock is the perfect time to do all these activities because I know the mailman comes at four. When I drop off my mail, I usually get to talk to the receptionist for a few minutes, who is typically one of the nicer people in the office.

3:45 PM As you can tell, it has been a "tough" day at work. At this point, my bowels finally say to me, "Thanks for the fast food, now please plop yourself on some porcelain." In other words, time to take a trip to the bathroom, my favorite place in the entire building. The bathroom is the only place in the office where you can be at peace. You don't have to talk to anyone, and you can finally put your stress aside and enjoy the moment, even if it may be a tad smelly.

Whenever I go to the toilet, I usually try to bring two things with me. First, I bring the sports page from the local newspaper. If I feel like I need to sit on the toilet for a while, then I will grab the business and life sections as well. If you have a cool office, you should find a copy of the sports page lying by the toilet. Of course, this rarely happened in my office.

The second object I bring with me is my Palm Pilot. I love the handheld for the ability to download great games for the crapper. My three favorite games for the toilet are two classics, Chess and Tetris, as well as Dope Wars. With Chess, I realize I'm no Bobby Fischer, but will I ever be able to get beyond level one? The computer is too damn good. I win less than 2% of the time and that isn't even including the number of times I have to reset the game because I know I'm going to lose! Dope Wars, on the other hand, is right up my alley. It is an economic-oriented drug game where the object is to maximize your income by buying and selling a variety of drugs in different cities within a month. While it is a game about drugs, to be successful you have to be financially savvy. At least that's what I tell myself.

4:30 PM Now that I am nearing the end of my workday, I begin to wrap up all my work and clean my desk. After accomplishing those tasks, I work my way back to ESPN.com to read the previews for the spotlighted games of the night. The biggest drawback to the West Coast is the early starting times for sporting events. I barely get to catch the second half of basketball games during the week because I come home too late, and on the weekends, football games start way before my head has recovered from the inevitable hangover.

5:00 PM The business world schedules meetings at five in order to keep you at work until the bitter end. Twice a week we have a meeting to discuss our company's financial performance and how we barely survived yet another round of lay-offs. It might sound strange, but part of me wishes that I would get laid-off and handed a six-month severance check. I mean, let's be real, the alternative is to get laid-off later anyway and probably receive a meager two-week severance. Every employee in a dot-com knows their time is coming anyway, so why not hope for the best? Severance pay in the dot-com era is a crapshoot. It almost all depends on how much money the company has left in the bank, more so than your position within the company, so you can only hope that your round of layoffs leaves you with a better deal than the guys who went before you or the poor saps whose time will undoubtedly arrive later on down the road.

5:45 PM The meeting ends and I run out of the office quicker than Michael Johnson in the 200 meters. On workdays when there are no meetings, I try to leave at times like 5:03 PM or 6:05 PM to show that I am not one of those guys that leaves exactly on the hour. As I leave, I walk down the hall and say "bye" to people who all I said was "hi" to nine hours earlier. I call them "Hibi's." All they do is confirm how lame and artificial the workplace can be in Corporate America.

6:04 PM I hop into my car knowing I have to sit in traffic for another hour. Great way to end a hard day of work, right? And no Stern.

7:00 PM Home sweet home! By the way, anyone hiring?

CHAPTER 3

"What the mind of man can conceive and believe, it can achieve."

—Napoleon Hill

Luckily for me, my weekend began early. I had taken Friday off because I was going to Las Vegas with my brothers for the weekend. Still, even when I was going out, I always had my work problems in the back of my mind. I just didn't know how to make a change, or more importantly, what to change to. I figured my brothers would offer some sound advice since they went through similar things when they were my age. Anyway, I had decided after work to meet up with some friends for a few drinks during happy hour to kick off my long weekend.

I was supposed to meet Jenny at Gordon Beirsch first. Brad and Jill were going to arrive a little later. They were all in their mid-twenties and worked corporate jobs which they weren't thrilled about either. I saw Jenny at an open table and joined her. After a few minutes of chitchat, the conversation got a tad more "juicy."

MIKE: What I'm telling you is that any girl can hook-up anytime she wants to at just about any bar.

JENNY: What are you talking about? And how do you define hook-up?

MIKE: Hook-up to me is just kissing, but in general, it means if you want to get laid you can.

JENNY: Okay, but what if the girl is ugly?

MIKE: It's a little tougher, but she will get plenty of nibbles if she is diligent. If she wants a catch, she'll definitely get one.

JENNY: A catch? What is this fishing?

MIKE: Yeah, like fishing.

JENNY: Women are fishermen?

MIKE: Yep.

JENNY: So you're saying that women are fishermen and that men are the fish that we are trying to catch?

MIKE: In a bar, women have the power to reel in almost any guy they want. They have the "equipment" to catch a fish, big or small, at a bar because we are fools for your bait. You can go after any fish you want, because you know a fish is going to be interested if you offer even a little taste of your bait. The question is what type of fish do you want to catch? And, what kind of bait must you use to catch that fish? Though for most fish, any bait will do.

JENNY: I'm not sure what type of fish I like at the bar. I'm not even sure how I'm supposed to use my bait, as you've so delicately termed it.

MIKE: Well, you should know there are rules to fishing, just like there are rules to dating.

JENNY: I can't wait to hear this.

MIKE: All right, first, you can't just catch any fish. Fish have to be a certain age and size for a fisherman to keep it. Otherwise they've got to throw it back. You always claim you don't like immature men, right?

JENNY: Yes, I like older men. But that doesn't mean they're mature.

MIKE: You also have to throw back many of the females due to population numbers.

JENNY: I'm not a lesbian!

MIKE: Okay…Okay…I just wanted to make sure you were listening…. When a fish sees some bait dangling in the ocean, he will do whatever he can to capture the treat. The fish will show you some of their swimmin' skills and try to ward off any other fish. He also has to be sly enough to escape the temptation of what might on first look be a decent meal but will in all likelihood evolve into a bad situation. There is always more food in the ocean.

JENNY: And the fish that has the most skill…well, least skill, is the one I'll catch?

MIKE: Depends. That's really up to you. How good you are at casting and reeling in. A good fisherwoman will haul in a fish that is more to her liking and won't have to bring home just any old catch. But make sure you realize the fish is only going for the food. They have no intention on being hooked. They know it's a dangerous endeavor, but they can't help but try for the quick score. But if your rod catches him, you know what that could ultimately lead to, right?

JENNY: Marriage…

MIKE: Yep. For better or for worse…

JENNY: I can't believe catching a fish and marriage are in the same sentence. Where do you get this stuff?

MIKE: I'm full of surprises! You want another beer?

JENNY: Yeah sure, Heineken.

MIKE: On the way to the bar, I'll look for some nice, tall, colorful fish for you. I know your type. You like tall lanky guys who are a little eccentric. I'll search for an electric eel, all right?

JENNY: Thanks for your help, but my rod is in the shop so I'm going to have to wait till the weekend to go fishing.

MIKE: Ha ha. I'll be back.

I walk up to the bar as Brad sees Jenny at our table.

BRAD: Hey Jenny, what's going on?

JENNY: Having a beer with Mike.

BRAD: Mind if I join you?

JENNY: I would mind if you didn't. What's up with you?

BRAD: I've been miserable. The season's over. I can't believe we lost our bowl game. To Fresno State of all teams. There's nothing worse than losing to one of those Cinderella story teams. I can take losing to a Florida State or a Miami, I even expect to sometimes. But Fresno State! Come on.

JENNY: I'm sorry. What was the score?

BRAD: 20-18. They missed a field goal as time expired. Needless to say, I'm not in the happiest of moods, so I guess the only thing I can do is drown my sorrow with many, many, beers. And a few shots.

JENNY: It's only football. How can you let it piss you off so much? It's only a sport. It doesn't really mean anything.

BRAD: Not today, Jenny. Not today.

JENNY: Why not? You shouldn't let it be that big of a deal.

BRAD: I don't really want to get into it, but I'm going to do every other guy in the world a favor and fill you in now, so that you never have to ask me, or any other pour soul, again. Tell all your lady friends as well.

JENNY: Okay.

BRAD: Imagine that you planned a big trip with your girlfriends once each year.

JENNY: Like *City Slickers*?

BRAD: Yeah, exactly, but every year, and you looked forward to the next one from the moment each trip ended. Say this year's trip happened to be going scuba diving in the Great Barrier Reef.

JENNY: God, I would love to go there!

BRAD: Okay, good. Well after months of researching for cheap fares, finding great hotels, training for scuba diving, and finally packing up for the big trip, you find out that a hurricane hit the reef and no one can visit the site until next year. All the energy, time, conversations, excitement, and emotional investment destroyed by just one event. Wouldn't you be pissed?

JENNY: That makes it a little more understandable, but there are so many games in football, how can one loss end the season?

BRAD: First, this was a bowl game, so it is the end of the world for this year no matter what. But even if it was the regular season, it's still the same thing. If you lose one game in college football, your whole season is probably over. Does it matter if the hurricane hits the day before your vacation or three weeks before if it means that your trip is ruined? In college football, a loss most likely means you can't win the National Championship. My trip is cancelled. Every year, I make a metaphorical hotel reservation for the National Championship game, and almost every year, I get hit by a hurricane. I put so much time into watching the recruiting scene, listening to interviews, reading articles, scouting other teams, watching the games, and just one loss ruins all my hopes, fun and dreams. Now, instead of going to the Great Barrier Reef, I end up having to go to the local beach down the road. And this year, even worse, it rains all week. Now do you see the big picture?

JENNY: I need to find you a girl who is just as crazy about sports as you are. I hear what you're saying, but I'm just not buying it. Sports are only a game. Vacations are real life. My life.

BRAD: All right fine, I'll try again to make it applicable to your life. How many times a year do you get your period?

JENNY: Excuse me?

BRAD: Go with me here. How many times?

JENNY: Fine. Twelve.

BRAD: Okay, and during each period you get really grumpy and have a lot of pains, but some are better than others, right?

JENNY: Yeah, for the most part.

BRAD: Well, in college football you play around 12 games a season. Each week is a period for a guy. The difference is that most of the time my periods go well because my team usually wins. Your period gets you in touch with your womanhood; my victories make me feel like a man. But if my school loses, well, then I highly recommend staying away from me for a while. My team usually loses two or three times a year, so that is at least a half a dozen times less than you and all your lady friends PMS, which lasts for days at a time, mind you. So you gals are allowed to be bitches maybe 10 times more a year than guys can be assholes. And even then, we're supposed to take it on the chin. As always, women are coming out ahead. I may sound bitter, but you asked.

JENNY: Please. You don't even know the half of it. You don't bleed as we do.

BRAD: Trust me, I bleed. On the inside, where it matters.

JENNY: Do you use tampons when your team loses as well?

BRAD: Okay, you got me there.

JENNY: I can't believe it! In the past 30 minutes, a football season has been compared to a period, and women have been described as fishermen trying to catch guys who are fish.

BRAD: Guys are fish? I thought we were dogs.

JENNY: You are! But Mike was saying that any women can hook-up anytime she wants to.

BRAD: That's true.

JENNY: Really? Maybe Mike isn't insane after all.

BRAD: Not even close. Where is Mike?

JENNY: He's still at the bar fighting to get a beer. He doesn't look happy about it at all.

BRAD: What's up with that date you went on last week? How did it go?

JENNY: Oh my god, don't get me started. It was horrible!

BRAD: Give me the details.

JENNY: Well, first, he's 30 minutes late to pick me up, then I had to pay for dinner, and later he tries to kiss me. Agghh!

BRAD: What do you mean you paid for dinner?

JENNY: He said he would pay for the movie tickets and that on the next date he would pay for a nice romantic dinner. He claimed he left his ATM card at home. He also said he doesn't like going to "nice" restaurants on first dates.

BRAD: Who is this guy?

JENNY: A big loser.

BRAD: Are you going on a second date? At least you'll get a romantic dinner, right?

JENNY: I don't think so...

BRAD: That's what I figured. I can't believe he made you pay. I would always pay on a first date.

JENNY: And I always would offer to split it.

BRAD: I think a girl should offer, although I will always refuse.

JENNY: Well, at least you're somewhat normal.

BRAD: So where, and how, did he try to kiss you?

JENNY: Well, we were supposed to go see a movie. I really wanted to see this independent film, but by that point in the date I just wanted to go home, so I recommended we rent a movie.

BRAD: You did what? Are you crazy?

JENNY: What? What did I do?

BRAD: You can't suggest renting a movie and watching it back home. That's like telling a guy he is going to get laid.

JENNY: Renting a movie?

BRAD: Yes, renting a movie! If any girl says that to me I'm thinking sex is a done deal. Signed, sealed, and delivered!

JENNY: You're disgusting.

BRAD: What movie did you rent?

JENNY: *Ferris Bueller's Day Off.* I hadn't seen the flick in awhile.

BRAD: Oh my god. You might as well have just come out and said, "I want to fuck."

JENNY: *Ferris Bueller*? What are you talking about?

BRAD: It's the perfect movie to skip. We all have seen the movie so many times that it's not a big deal to miss a few scenes. If the guy is lucky, he will have you before Ferris and Cameron pick up Ferris' girlfriend in front of the principal at their school. You can't rent a movie like that. If you rent a movie at all, it's got to be a serious drama that neither of you have seen. No horror, no comedy, got it?

JENNY: Yeah, I think so.

BRAD: Well, how were you guys sitting?

JENNY: We sat next to each other on the couch, not fully cuddled but close.

BRAD: Well, no wonder he made a move. The guy's gotta try.

JENNY: Great, now you're on his side. He made a move, I said no, so we watched until the end and then he left.

BRAD: I'm sorry that it didn't go well, but at least you now know about the movie rental rule. Chalk it up as a learning experience.

JENNY: Just another chapter in my lifelong horror story with men. I think I'm already on Volume Two. Anyway, whatever happened with that little girl you were chatting with at the bar last week. Anything happening from that?

BRAD: Yeah, we hooked-up.

JENNY: So you like her!

BRAD: No, I'm deciding whether or not I should be nice and give her my token call or just be a dick and not call her at all. Typical guy problem. There's never a satisfactory solution.

JENNY: She must have been interesting. You guys talked all night.

BRAD: She was interesting to get, but not to know.

JENNY: I hate guys.... At least you're not a total dirtball. What turned you off?

BRAD: Well, the minute we hooked up I knew it was over.

JENNY: Why? This should be good.

BRAD: I can't go out with a girl who isn't a challenge. Now that I've scored, I'll only be thinking with my dick and not my head. I won't really want to get to know her, I'll just want to get in her.

JENNY: So what's a girl to do if she likes a guy?

BRAD: Well, if there is potential, she should hold out at least a little while. But I'll only give a girl so much time before I better see some solid action. If I'm not getting laid by the end of the first month, see ya. No bang, no hang.

JENNY: I'm going to throw up. How can men think like that? Why do women like guys?

BRAD: Because we're simple and easy to understand; that's what makes men great. But guys have the reverse problem. While we obviously want to get into a girl's pants, we know that if we like them we should probably just get their phone number. Otherwise, our mentality is completely warped towards the short-term. So, it's either she becomes a number or you get her number.

JENNY: Funny…very funny.

BRAD: Thanks.

JENNY: But, you know, I don't usually give my number at the bar anymore. Now, I only give my email address. I've had a few stalkers.

BRAD: Good old email. I have had plenty of experiences playing the email game.

JENNY: Really? What's your take on email versus the phone?

BRAD: Just as you said, it's a smart safety factor. I don't mind if a girl gives me her email. But I better get the number after my first email. Otherwise, it's "Adios, Chica!" The problem with email is that once you start emailing, expectations increase too fast because communication is easier.

JENNY: What do you mean?

BRAD: With the phone it might be once or twice a week early on in the relationship to setup plans and stuff. But with email, you're always connected, especially if you work in an office. It's easier to communicate more frequently. If you start emailing with each other, the expectation of frequent communication increases too quickly for the relationship to handle.

JENNY: And that leads to what?

BRAD: I don't know what it leads to, but that explains why I would rather use the phone. Still, at some point, you learn the girl's email address anyway. So, maybe it's a wash. The problem is that there are too many unknowns early in the relationship. There is no balance of power, and email just makes the game that much more difficult. The game is so much fun, though.

JENNY: I know the game can go on forever on the phone, but when does the email game end?

BRAD: I guess it's the same with email. At some point, you've gotta balance your communication needs and realize the expectations in the relationship. The truth of the matter, though, is that if you like each other, it will work out eventually.

Jill walks to the table and grabs a seat.

JENNY: Hey Jill, what's going on?

JILL: Hey guys, this seat open?

BRAD: Yeah, grab a seat. Mike is at the bar. Finally, the whole gang is here.

JENNY: What took you so long to get here?

JILL: I was watching Clinton's speech on television. God, he is so hot for someone that age.

JENNY: I know. The man just has some sort of power over women. I wish I could have interned at the White House while he was president.

JILL: Monica was so lucky.

BRAD: You guys don't think Clinton is a dirtball?

JENNY: Of course he is. He's a guy. But he has this intriguing power over me. I think most women feel the same way.

BRAD: Are you ladies saying that if you interned you would have had a little affair in the Oval Office as well?

JENNY: For sure! I'm not a fan of cigars though!

BRAD: Really. That's amazing. I've seen girls go both ways on Bill. Some hate him, some love him. What about Bush?

JILL: No freaking way, but I would definitely have taken Lincoln!

JENNY: Lincoln? Really? I do love the beard and the hat. It would be rather nice to cuddle up with Mr. Lincoln.

BRAD: No way. He wasn't good looking at all.

JENNY and JILL: It's not all about looks!

BRAD: What about George Washington?

JENNY: Not really into him.

JILL: He's not my type either.

BRAD: How can you not want GW, but want Lincoln? I just don't get it.

JILL: He's Honest Abe, and that is more than enough for me these days.

BRAD: What other presidents would you bang?

JENNY: Obviously, JFK.

BRAD: Obviously.

JILL: I'd have taken Reagan home for the night when he was in his prime. He was a movie star!

BRAD: What about Adams?

JENNY: Nah, I'm not a 1700's type of girl.

JILL: I would go for Andrew Jackson.

BRAD: Why him? He was supposed to be an arrogant son of a bitch.

JILL: I can just tell from his picture on the $20 bill that he was confident. He looks like he would be good in bed.

BRAD: You can tell that by the way he looks on a $20 bill? And you say guys are crazy.

JILL: Money talks, baby!

BRAD: Whatever. Speaking of looking confident, my good old friend is coming back. What's with the big smile?

JENNY: I'm not sure, but I know we're going to find out.

I walk back to the table with four beers. That's just the type of guy I am! How much would it have sucked if I returned with only two beers? You always gotta keep abreast of all developments and keep an eye on the entire playing field. That's exactly why I make a great point guard.

MIKE: Hey guys!

JENNY: What happened over there? I saw a little conversation happening with that girl at the bar.

MIKE: I saw Brad talking to you, so I figured I had a few minutes to work my magic.

JENNY: Anything good come of it?

MIKE: I'll put it this way. Brad, I'm going to need a wingman tonight!

BRAD: What's the low down? Give me the scoop.

MIKE: The girl I was talking to at the bar worked with me at my last job. She said there's a party tonight and she thinks it could be crazy. She's usually on target about this stuff.

BRAD: What time do you want to go?

MIKE: Not sure. It's Thursday, so I figure we get there around eleven.

BRAD: That's cool. Let's go home, shower up, and then head to the party.

MIKE: Ladies, are you interested in joining us tonight?

JENNY: I can't. I have a meeting at eight in the morning. Who schedules a meeting on Friday at eight?

JILL: Your boss, I guess. What a dick. I'm too tired. I'm going to go home and get some sleep.

BRAD: Well, looks like we can be dirtballs tonight, Mike. No one we know is going to be there.

MIKE: You read my mind.

We finished our conversation and beer. I headed home to get ready for the house party.

CHAPTER 4

"The path to success is to take massive, determined action."

—Anthony Robbins

Almost everyone would agree with the following statements. Men are less sensitive than women. Men are often incapable of expressing their true feelings because they keep all their emotions bottled up inside. Men do not know how to listen. And, finally, men are too logical in their decision-making processes.

It is the opposite qualities of women that, in my opinion, drive many females to keep a diary. Women are able to express their deepest thoughts and desires in their diaries without any opposing opinion. The diary listens and never talks. What women don't understand is that, contrary to their hard held belief, men also listen, they just don't usually agree. Women always want to know what men think, and men hate being asked to sally forth with their thoughts because they know their response will fail to evoke happiness or satisfaction. In fact, men know it will far more likely evoke sadness and strife. If you disagree, whether you're a man or women, please raise your hand. I didn't think so.

The startling truth is that in many ways women are more logical than men. When men go out for the night rational behavior or logic does not motivate them, but rather by sexual impulse. To put it bluntly, men go after whatever women are available. Their actions are usually based on carnal desires. When women go out, they usually think logically about whether if they should hook up with a guy they are talking to at a bar. Thoughts such as, "Will he or my friends think I'm a slut?" Or "I will only kiss him, and will do no more," are always in the back of a woman's mind. Women, not men, are the ones trapped by logic. However, when it comes to making decisions with a long-term impact like marriage or moving in together, the tables turn and men become the more logical gender. But isn't it wise to think those decisions through more carefully since there are larger ramifications at stake?

In light of the above and the great confusion caused by our very evident differences, I offer the following gift to the fairer sex in an attempt to bridge the gap of understanding that stands between us. Women, here is your chance to see what men do and think when they go out to a party. If you were to read my journal, the entry below would describe my night at the house party.

December XX, 2000

8:30 PM Showered up. Cleaned my room and made my bed. If I bring a girl back, I have to at least make her believe that I'm tidy (Hopefully, she doesn't use my bathroom).

9:00 PM Brad arrived at my house while I pulled up MapQuest to find, to my pleasant surprise, that the party was only a 15-minute walk away. Sweet! No waiting and paying for a cab. Waiting for a cab in San Francisco can take forever. It's not as cold as Chicago or New York, so cabs aren't at your footsteps all the time.

9:05 PM One shot of tequila each.

9:08 PM One shot of tequila each.

9:10 PM Three games of FIFA Soccer on PlayStation. The rules of the game are one shot of tequila for every goal scored against, and two shots for the loser. I never lose in FIFA, so within 25 minutes Brad is already wasted. The beauty of men and video games is that, when you mix the two, you experience this peak of intensity and competitiveness for the 15 minutes or so that the game lasts. Then, as soon as the game ends you go back to being best friends.

9:55 PM My brother Jon called and we confirmed plans to meet at the Mirage in Las Vegas tomorrow.

10:15 PM Sprayed cologne on most body areas. Even "Mr. Friendly" wants to smell good (On the boxers not the body part).

10:30 PM A shot of tequila right before we headed out. I wanted to make sure that I was as drunk as possible at the party. No way in the world do I want to be the only sober one there. Isn't that a sign of an alcoholic? If it is, then almost all men are one.

11:00 PM We entered the party. It was in an upstairs apartment/house. The party was happening. First rule for men is to go straight to the alcohol. A man feels naked at a party without a beer in his hand. The keg was in the back, which provided an opportunity for a preliminary walk through. I glanced at a few women, said hi a few times, and made my way back to the alcohol corner.

When you first walk into a party, you have to be like the Terminator, scoping out the situation and reading everyone's profiles. With regard to other guys, well you pass by the guys. For girls, you must immediately assess several factors. First, are they attractive? If they are attractive, do they have a boyfriend? If they are attractive and do not have a boyfriend, do they seem approachable? If they are approachable, what do I say? If I don't know what to say, what can I use to my advantage (friend, keg, liquor, cigarette, clothing, lighter, or sports game)? If I don't have anything to capitalize on, how can I avoid her till later when I'm in a groove? It's literally like the scientific method. You take one step at a time, until the end, where you assess the results, develop a hypothesis and go after a certain lady.

11:15 PM I noticed a girl who was pumping the keg, which gave me two minutes tops to start a conversation. That's all you need at a party. I'm never good with pickup lines, so I started with the easy, "What type of beer is it?" Nothing pretty, no harm done. It got her attention though. She was decent looking, definitely bangable, but certainly not my priority. She would be my Mariano Rivera, my closer, but only if I needed it. We babbled for a few, and then I told her I needed to go see my friend to deliver the beer.

11:30 PM Brad and I conducted our customary walk around, and noticed that we knew no one there. My friend from the bar ended up not showing. She had said that she would know most of the people there, and I counted on her to act as my entree into the social circle. Newman! We decided to head into the living room and we started chatting with these two girls. Not that it's easy, my friend did most of the work, but it was obvious that these girls wanted to talk. All men know which females want to talk, and well, which ones are bitches. Conversation was going well with these girls, but it was too early to successfully score. It was like scoring a quick goal in soccer and then allowing your mindset to shift from attacking to playing defense. If you let that happen and the other team scores, i.e. another guy steals the girl away, it's impossible to get back on your feet. It happens all the time. I told Brad that I was going to grab some more beer.

12:00 AM I decided to get a Jack & Coke instead, and coincidentally, I ran into three girls at the liquor bar. I was having a decent conversation with the ladies, trying to angle myself towards the woman I thought I liked the most, meaning the one I was most likely to bang, and it seemed to be working. Then she left with her friends to go continue mingling. I figured one of two things happened. Possibility 1: I was alone and didn't have my wingman to support me. It's very difficult to score in a 3-on-1 situation. It's just too difficult to isolate one of the girls. Possibility 2: She may have not been into me. It was a boring conversation in hindsight, and I wasn't happy about the fact that she might have thought I was boring. I suddenly realized that I was becoming too introspective. I do this too much as it is, and it can definitely do me no good whatsoever when I'm aiming for a hook-up. At a party, you have to be ruthless. Let introspection take over when you're sitting in front of the tube watching football.

12:25 AM I returned to my friend, who gave me a look that seemed to say, "Where the hell did I go?" He was right. I should have come back immediately, but I thought he could handle the other two girls for a while. He was running the show before anyway. I had an opportunity with three girls, and well, he had an opportunity with two girls. Either way, I knew I was just making excuses for myself and should have come back earlier. I could tell the flame had died. These two girls were a lost cause, at least for tonight. Oh well, live and learn. Must move on.

12:45 AM At this point, I started to get a little frustrated. I had a few conversations with girls, the only reason to go to a party (other than drinking other people's beer), and no attempt was anywhere near successful. I had no telephone numbers, no emails, and no vibes. I had my few token conversations with guys, buying time until I ran into another girl. After expounding the argument that the Big-10 is better than the Pac-10 for the fifth time at the party, I needed to take a cigarette break. Brad doesn't smoke, so I went out alone.

1:00 AM I went to the smoker's corner in the back of the house. I'm a big fan of the smoker's corner. In a way, it unites people who have similar interests, smoking that is, but it also offers an easy place to talk, much easier than inside. I don't know if it's mental, but I seem to have better luck outside than inside at house parties.

"Do you have a lighter?" A girl on the back porch said to me. There were probably about eight people back there, but for some reason this girl was somewhat alone, or so it seemed when filtered through my "guy vision." I always have a lighter. A lighter is like the American Express Card at a party, "Don't Leave Home Without It." I can't tell you how many times a lighter has led me to a "quality" night, or at the least an interesting conversation. Sure, I do the work, but the flame ignites the conversation, so to speak. What if you don't smoke? Doesn't matter. Always carry a lighter. Tell her that your buddy gave it to you to hold, or that you're a social smoker, or that you quit one hour ago. Whatever works. A lighter is an opportunity, and you don't get many of them at a party or anywhere else for that matter. "Yeah, sure, let me find it in my pocket," I said. Of course, I found my cigarettes first. That way we could smoke together and have a few more minutes to chat.

1:20 AM I was already smashed. She was having a good time with me and things seemed to be going well. I knew after 20 minutes that I had the vibe. What is the vibe, you might ask? The vibe is like an energy field that you can feel between yourself and someone else. You can't actually see it, but you both know there is some energy floating around from the other person that is creating a strangely pleasant feeling. It's similar to when you hop onto a broken escalator; you can still feel the energy field from the machine, even though it's not moving. Add in a lot of sexual spice, and you got the something far better. When you have a vibe, you should become more aggressive in executing your game. I usually try to touch a girl on her wrists or hands, maybe even place my hand on her shoulder if we laugh about something. Now that I knew I could get lucky, I had to do something about it. I love having the vibe. It's a great feeling because no matter what she's thinking, at least I think I can get laid. It doesn't even matter what she thinks. The vibe was there and my juices were flowing.

1:30 AM The party was starting to wind down, so we went inside into the kitchen where the remnants, destroyed, hopefuls and hangers-on, were still hanging out. I wasn't really thrilled about going inside, because now I didn't have her isolated. Therefore, I had to strategize a plan. She went to the toilet, which gave me an opportunity to talk with my buddy. I told him I had a vibe going with this girl, and asked him if he cared if I left with her. Brad didn't care at all, but warned me that I better score, and that he wanted to hear the details. She came back to the kitchen, and in front of the entire group said, "Well, I guess I'm going to be heading out. I have to go find my jacket in the other room." In my mind, it was an invitation. Maybe I was right and maybe I was wrong, but I had to find the balls to find out. I told my buddy right at that moment that if I didn't say anything now, it was over and I blew my opportunity. I had to step up to the plate. If you don't ask the question, you'll never find out the answer. So I walked across the hall and I asked her if she could give me a ride home. She said, "Not a problem. Where do you live?" I deflected that question since it was an easy walk home, by responding that I needed to say a quick bye to my friend.

1:45 AM We headed downstairs and she put her arm around me. She put her arm around me! I felt like she was forcing the issue. Like a man. Why would I care though? The arm around the shoulder told me I was "in." We both knew it, but now I knew she really wanted it. We hopped in her car and she drove to my place. We parked and started to hook-up. It was starting to get very intense, my hands were up her shirt, and she was feeling my cock, when she suddenly stopped and said, "What did you say to your friend about me?" Are you kidding me? Was this girl getting serious already? I didn't think it could have been more obvious that this was going to be a one-night stand. She was actually a lot older, in her thirties, thank you very much, and I could tell that she had done this many of times before. Some things just don't need to be said. As we all know, communication is 90% non-verbal. I answered in a confident manner,

"Honestly, I said to him I thought I had a vibe with you, and I told him that I might leave without him." I think she was impressed by my honesty. I guess that honesty thing does work after all. She leaned over and we started kissing again.

2:15 AM At this point, it had been like 15-20 minutes kissing in the car, so I said to her, "You want to go upstairs?" I love kissing, but it does get tiresome when there is much more to do and a lot more fun to be had. She stopped kissing me, sat back in the driver seat and thought about the proposition I just made. Give me a break. I knew she was coming up. She was totally putting on an act to make herself look like a "good-girl." Honey, that act is done. Very few girls drive you home, put their arm around you, start kissing in the car in your driveway, let you play with their breasts and then refuse to go inside. Would you disagree? Anyway, she said something like, "Let me think about it for a few more minutes." That was a little annoying but I knew it was only a matter of time. She started kissing me again. Lucky for me, I'm an excellent kisser. Two minutes later, she whispered into my ear the words every guy longs to hear, "We should go up." Now, I only had to close the deal.

2:30 AM We were up in my bedroom now, and by this point I was already ready for dessert. This did not stand well since we hadn't even gotten to the main course yet. She wasn't a good kisser at all. She was always on a different page than me. When my lips were open, her lips were closed. When I wanted to kiss her softly, she became aggressive. I don't think she realized that her tongue could actually move.

We started to have sex. I felt like I was just getting my groove on, and nothing more. But that was fine. Either way, I still got laid, which meant I probably did better than 99% of the men that went out last night.

4:45 AM We both passed out.

6:00 AM I didn't realize that 30-year old women can still traverse the "Walk of Shame," just like girls back in college. She had to leave early in the morning to be at some event. The funny thing was that my roommates didn't get back home from their night out until 5:30 AM, so they were still sitting on the couch chatting about their own drink-inflated evening when she was getting up. Therefore, for her to leave she would have to saunter down the "Walk of Shame." While for me it would turn out to be the "Walk of Fame." You know, that moment when your buddies sit there, staring wide-eyed and mouths agape, barely managing a grunt of acknowledgement, while the gal who just left your bedroom makes her way as quickly as possible without running, head somewhat downturned, allowing just a moment of eye contact and forcing a quick, embarrassed smile. All the while, you lean against the opening of the doorway to your bed-room and watch the spectacle unfold, a cigarette dangling from your mouth to complete the scene. I gloated with my roommates for the next hour. Before she left, we exchanged phone numbers, but we both knew that was the end of it. She didn't live in the city, so it made the new relationship very difficult. Maybe it could have been a differ-ent story if she lived nearby. Instead of a one-night stand, it could have been something more, like a six-month stand.

7:00 AM I crashed and tried to get some sleep before my trip to Las Vegas. My flight was in the afternoon, which meant even odds that I wouldn't oversleep.

FRIDAY

CHAPTER 5

*"If you are not an idealist by the time you are twenty you
have no heart, but if you are still an idealist by the time you
are thirty, you don't have a head."*

—Randolph Bourne

I met two of my older brothers at the airport, Mark and Ben, and
waited at the gate until the plane was ready to board. I have a whole
slew of brothers; there are five of us in all, only eight years apart in
total. I'm the youngest of the bunch. Ben headed to the bathroom for
a few minutes after eating a few greasy hamburgers from
McDonald's.

Mark was paying a lot of attention to these two ladies who were
irate over the fact that they would have to wait three hours for the
next flight because they got bumped from their original flight. I was
reading the newspaper, minding my own business, having seen the
same thing happen many times before. I used to work for an airline.
In fact, I worked for the department that overbooks flights; so seeing
people go crazy at the airport was just another day for me. People
have no clue about the economic process of overbooking flights, not
that they would be any calmer if they did. Still, your average traveler

is under the mistaken impression that overbooking is random, that it's a matter of bad luck. It isn't.

"Mike, I hate seeing people get bumped from flights. If I buy a ticket for that plane at that time, there should be no reason why I don't get on that flight. Why can't airlines figure out that all overbooking does is piss off their customers?"

"It does a lot more than that for them."

"What does that mean?"

"It pisses a few people off, no doubt, and it also makes the industry billions of dollars every year. Take my word for it."

"Okay, so you're playing the experience card. That's cool."

"Well, I may be younger, but on this occasion I know something that you don't."

"Let's hear it. I never really paid attention anyway when you blabbed on about what you did at Acme Airlines, so here's your chance to strut your stuff. How does overbooking benefit the industry? If I'm sold, first round in Vegas is on me."

"You're so generous. Drinks in Vegas are free."

"That's the type of brother I am!"

"Okay, listen up. You've got to realize that airlines, like any industry, are dictated by the most basic economic principle; supply and demand. Every company has to manage the supply and demand of their product or they will fail, right? Take movies. Matinees are cheaper because less people go, so the way to stimulate demand for the earlier showings is to lower the price. In a way, this is a solid analogy. Movies and airlines are actually pretty similar on this count. Once a movie is shown, a theater can't make any more money on that showing. As soon as a flight takes off, an airline can't make any more money from that flight."

"Yeah, I'm with you. Like D.C. Metro, where you pay more during rush hours."

"Basically the same type of thing. Economics is mostly common sense if you really think about it anyway."

"So how does this relate to overbooking?"

"All right, next you've got to realize that the passenger sitting next to you sometimes pays five times more for essentially the same ticket. Everyone on the plane pays a different price, and the airline determines who pays what based on their advance purchase requirements and inventory control."

"I'm aware of that. You mean like 7,14, or 21 days before your flight takes off."

"Yeah, exactly. That's how the airline manages the passenger mix. The analyst wants to ensure both leisure and business travelers are accounted for. Business travelers usually buy their tickets within 21 days and therefore pay more money. They have to go, so they pay the extra dough."

"They pay for flexibility?"

"Exactly. Actually, many flights are unprofitable and only fly because they provide a more flexible schedule for the business traveler."

"How do you actually manage all this information?"

"The airline has software programs that analyze tons of data to interpret the best strategy to handle the passenger mix. Unfortunately, it isn't perfect and that's where the human-side comes into play. People are needed to 'fix' the computer error."

"I guess that's why Kirk is Captain of the Enterprise instead of Spock. You need the human element. Incidentally, this is exactly why college football should put more weight on the AP polls than on the computer rankings in the BCS. Those are totally bogus. Just had to get that in there. Anyway, you were saying that there's an element of error. How much are we talking about?"

"Why do you always gotta bring up your Star Trek crap. You're such a geek. But to answer your question, there's a lot of error. There's a whole department for that alone. That was why my first job was cool. The work I did actually had a direct effect on the bottom line. It was just a little boring after a while. The benefits were killer though. Flying around whenever I wanted was definitely hard to give up."

"I'm sure. Free tickets anywhere! That's major leverage for making way with the ladies. You should have used those flying benefits to your advantage. Girls love to travel."

"I did. Trust me, I did."

"When? I never heard anything aside from getting one girl's phone number. Keyword being one."

"Shut up dude. Don't undersell my accomplishments…. I got digits twice."

"Okay, it was two, but no good stories came from either one."

"Where've you been? I dated one girl for a while. You knew about that, right?"

"Not sure…what was her name?"

"Alice."

"Oh, you mentioned her to me. I think that was during my residency. I was so busy then that the only thing I remember from those days was my pager number. What happened again?"

❧   ❧   ❧

It was a Thursday after work and I was meeting up with some friends at John Barleycorn in Chicago. Barleycorn is the king of yuppie bars in Chicago. It's in Lincoln Park. Having landed a "God Spot" right in front of the place, I arrived at the bar a little before my friends. I headed right into the bar. No one sane meets outside in Chicago. I looked around the room. It was the time at a bar where either you grab a table immediately, or you stand the rest of the night. I wanted a table, so I grabbed a seat near the back end of the bar where my friends could see me without having to hunt around. The waitress came over and I ordered an Amstel Light. You normally won't catch a guy sucking down a light beer, but for some reason Amstel Light doesn't carry the normal "light beer" stigma.

Two girls were chatting away at the table next to me, which made me feel like a bit of a loser—all alone, sitting at a table at a bar. I was anxiously hoping for one of my friends to show up. One of the girls left her seat to go to the bathroom, so I had an opportunity to get a good look at the other girl. Incredibly, it turned out to be the same girl who had been sitting a couple rows in front of me at the Cubs game a couple of days earlier.

This girl was beautiful. She easily could have been mistaken for a Victoria Secret's model. She had silky dark hair down to her shoulders, long legs, and entrancing green eyes. I couldn't stop looking into her eyes. I know girls always complain when guys stare at them excessively, but in this case, I couldn't help myself. My animal instincts were too powerful. I had to look at her. My brain gave me no choice.

Why do girls mind if men stare at them anyway? I would take it as a compliment if a girl couldn't take her eyes off of me. That way at least I would know if she thought I was handsome and might be interested to talk. I guess for women it's so much easier. All a woman has to do is walk to the other end of the bar, turn her head, and see how many men look her way as she walks by. If there are at least a few, she is attractive. Men, on the other hand, have to put on their jacket, find the nearest ATM machine, and print out their bank account balance. If it's high, they're in business.

Luckily, having seen her at the Cubs game, I had an easy conversation starter.

"You were at the Cubs game against the Pirates on Tuesday, right?" She was a little surprised that I was talking to her, not to mention that I knew where she was this past Tuesday.

"Yes I was. How did you know that?" She didn't seem entirely impressed, and I realized that I had just taken a major risk. My first foray into conversation, and she was already convinced that I was stalking her.

"I sat a couple rows behind you on the first base side."

I didn't mention the fact that I stared at her between every pitch, as well as during "Take Me Out To The Ball Game." If that song has never given me anything throughout all the years and all my baseball games (which it has, but just for argument's sake), on that night it provided me with something very special. As everyone stood to sing, I was offered an unobstructed view of her legs. At the risk of repeating myself, they were perfect. I have a love-hate relationship with seeing beautiful women at sporting events. I totally want to concentrate on the game, but I want sex all the time. What's a man to do? I'll tell you what you do. During the spring/summer season, after girls emerge from hibernation and start showing some skin, go to a baseball game, stand behind the most beautiful women you can find, and shamelessly stare and dream.

"Oh, no way! What a game!" Recovery!

"It was awesome. The Cubbies might do it this year. They just might." They won't, but everyone in Chicago likes to believe it.

"I try not to miss any games anymore now that the race is so tight. It's so exciting."

"Do you have a season package or something?"

"My girlfriends and I got a season package together. We split the games. Do you go to a lot of games?"

This could be better than I had even imagined. Not only does she like sports, but she has girlfriends that like sports as well. Let me say that again. She has *girlfriends* that like sports. If I hook this up, I will be a living legend among my guy friends for at least the next few months.

"I do my best. I've been to six games this year. Every game is a blast."

"Not bad." This girl is still actually talking to me. We're talking about baseball! She's staying on my turf. All good. "I'm a little nervous. The Cubbies got us exactly where they want us."

"Where's that?"

"They're playing well enough to be in contention, but not good enough to win the pennant."

Holy crap, this girl isn't fooling around. "Tell me about it. Being a Cubs fan is an exercise in pain and torture. You come to Barleycorn a lot?"

"I live nearby, so it's convenient for me. It isn't my favorite bar, though."

Do we go to bars merely because we want to satisfy our urge as social animals to avoid the feeling that we are no more than hermits who just hide out in their shells? Doesn't it seem like half the people you know these days go to bars that they don't even want to go to from the start? Don't you find it weird when a group hangs out together at a friend's apartment, chatting for a few hours, and then goes to the bar and talks to no one but themselves? Shouldn't the group just stay at home, have a good time there, and save the $30 they'll each spend on shots? Why do we feel it's necessary to go to the bar on the weekends? In college, you had to go out to be part of the scene. Once you leave college, though, you rarely know anyone at the bars anymore. Life isn't *Cheers*.

"I like this bar, but the crowd gets a little old after a while."

"You're definitely right about that. Do you live nearby too?" This isn't the question I generally like to hear.

"I live just off of Lincoln. Not too far away."

"Where on Lincoln?"

Damn, she blew my cover. I lived just outside the unwritten line, demarcated by Irving Park, that separates the "cool" pads from the "average" ones. My place was fine. It had plenty of parking and reasonable rent, but I knew that the mere mention of the location of my apartment diminished my likelihood of nailing this girl. Just by mentioning a neighborhood that you live in, you are immediately classified into a certain mold. The only way to break that mold is to prove them wrong. Unfortunately, most people don't give you that chance. So you've got to learn to deal with your stereotype, and you've got to learn how to overcome it when necessary.

"Irving and Lincoln."

"Oh…do you like it?" Not the response I wanted to hear, but what did I expect?

"Yeah, it's cool. The rent is good. It's easy to park, and it's 5-10 minutes away from the heart of Lincoln Park. Also, it saves me a lot of time when I go to work." Notice how I slipped the last part into the equation. Remember how I just said you've got to learn how to overcome stereotypes.

"Where do you work?" I'm good to go now. Please fasten your seatbelts and prepare for take-off.

"I work for Acme Airlines."

"No way! That's awesome! What do you do for them?" Easy money. I'll tease her and play around a little bit.

"I'm a stewardess."

"Really? You don't look gay." Wow, that was straightforward. This chick has some pizzazz. I can work with that.

"No, I'm just screwing around. I overbook flights."

"So you're the bastard that screws everyone." Everything was going as planned.

"Yep. I'm the one."

"Do you get to fly around for free and stuff? I heard airline employees get to do that."

"I got back from New Zealand with a friend just last week."

"Oh my god! I want your job. How long did you go for?"

"The weekend. I took Friday off."

"You went to New Zealand for the weekend. I go to my parent's house for the weekend. I'm so jealous."

"Did I mention that I get to sit first class? My seat to New Zealand turned into a bed. Filet mignon on the way there, lobster on the way back."

"Showoff! I've never flown first class. You're so lucky...and spoiled."

"Yeah, I probably am. That's the benefit of a cool job."

"Where else have you been?"

"You know, the usual. Amsterdam, New Orleans, Hawaii, Las Vegas, San Francisco, London." I was milking it for all it was worth.

"I heard that buddies get to travel for free." I was just waiting for her to say that. Time to go in for the kill.

"Not free, but damn cheap."

"So where are you going to take your new buddy?" I was, as they say in the movie *Swingers*, money!

"Where do you want to go? By the way, my name is Mike. What's your name?"

"Alice...I would die to go to Hawaii and Paris."

"Well, here's my phone number. My friend just walked in and gestured for me to leave. Sometimes you gotta do what you don't want to do." This is as smooth as I get.

"That being what?"

"Leave, and stop talking to you. Listen, give me a call next week if you'd like to climb a volcano or eat some Brie. I'm sure I could arrange something."

"Don't worry, you'll be getting my call sometime soon."

"I hope so. Have a fun night."

I didn't even care that she was more into my job's benefits than she was into me. It's always a great sign if a girl is going to make the first call. These days, a young guy has to use whatever he can to "snag" a quality woman. Some guys might wear tight clothing to show off their physique in order to attract women. Other guys might have a unique style of dress or a sexy accent. Many men capitalize on their power, money, or prestige to get ahead with the ladies. Some guys even try to use their personalities. The passport to where I hoped to get that night happened to be the benefits of my job. Sometimes, just sometimes, jobs aren't that bad after all.

❧   ❧   ❧

"So you went to Paris together, right?"

"Yeah, we went on one date and then we went to Paris and Hawaii together, back-to-back weekends. It was crazy!"

"That's awesome. I can't believe I don't remember that girl. So how did it end?"

"I ran out of buddy passes."

"She used you."

"Yep. It was totally worth it."

"Nothing wrong with getting used by a woman."

"As long as you're getting laid, right?"

"You've learned well young Jedi…. Now finish telling me about overbooking."

"Not a problem. How many people do you think don't show up for a given flight?"

"I don't know, 5% maybe."

"Try 15%. 15% of people on average don't show up for their flight even though they purchased a ticket."

"Are you serious? It's that high? People just lose their money?"

"No, they don't necessarily lose their money. People miss a flight for a variety of reasons. Leisure travelers like you and I very rarely miss a plane. That's why you think the no-show rate is so low. But business people are always missing planes, changing dates, or going on a later flight. It happens all the time, and the airlines know that."

"So the airline overbooks flights on average by 15% to compensate for the fact that 15% of passengers don't show up. That way they make more money. Seems to make sense. But if less than 15% no-show then a few people will get bumped. That's what happened with those girls at the counter, right?"

"You got it! Except you're missing one thing. Maybe, the most important thing. There is actually a reason that people should get upset, which is this. The airlines don't actually overbook at the 15% level. They overbook until a denied boarding, as they say in the industry, costs the airline more than it receives from the additional revenue of another passenger. And since any additional passenger who purchases a ticket close to take-off pays a lot of money for that ticket, they will consistently overbook over and above the 15% barrier."

"Okay, now that's ridiculous. They shouldn't be allowed to do that. The airlines are just screwing people over. They're totally exploiting us and inconveniencing tons of people."

"Whoa. Chill out, dude. It's not as bad as it seems, although everyone seems to have a story. That's because people in general always will remember the worst thing that happened to them. People don't like to get burned."

"Why is it not as bad as it seems?"

"Well, for one, sometimes the no-show rate is above 15%, so despite over-over booking, the flight still didn't have any denied boardings. Secondly, the airlines make bank using this strategy. It costs them almost nothing for a denied boarding. At most, a free flight or a couple hundred bucks. Third, most people don't mind getting bumped because they pocket the money from the voucher simply for waiting a couple of hours. It's totally worth it if you have the time because you know you're going to fly again. Finally, for the amount of people that do fly, the percentage of people who get denied boarded is really small. Most flights aren't even full."

"You make a pretty good case. But it still bothers me that they take advantage of people like that. The bottom line is that almost every time I fly I see some customer arguing with one of the gate agents. Airline customer service is horrible."

"Airline customer service does suck. Dude, you're a doctor. Doctor's offices do the same thing. People cancel their appointments all the time. Now, you see doctors charging a patient if they miss their appointment on the premise that there time is valuable. It's the same thing."

"Yeah, but doctor offices don't overbook."

"True. Fine. Let me give you another example. When it's closer to home, the idea of overbooking really starts to sink in. Did you know that your buddy Tim overbooks seats at his theater all the time?"

"Really?"

"Yep. Here's what he does. Let's say you owned a theater and were showing an incredible play that was selling out every show. You had two parts to the theater, assigned seats and open seating. When you looked into the theater during the actual shows, you realized that on average 50 people in the open seating section were not showing up even though they purchased a ticket."

"Okay."

"For simplicity's sake, let's say there are 1,000 open section seats at $100 a pop for each show. Therefore, the play would bring in revenue of $100,000 on open seating if the play sold out."

"All right. And since 50 seats are empty each play that would mean I could potentially earn another $5,000 every damn day if I decided to overbook the show."

"You're getting the idea. If you overbooked the play by only 1%, you would earn an additional $1,000 every day. Then, you would have to subtract the cost to your production if everyone showed up for the play. Let's say it was $750, $75 for each of the 10 people that you overbooked. The thing to remember though is that most likely everyone will get to watch the play, despite the overbooking, because the theater no-show rate is 5% and you're only overbooking by 1%."

"Basically, I'm easily making six-figures solely on overbooking. That's pure cash in my pocket. Pretty impressive."

"Now, just magnify those numbers to reflect the billion dollar airline industry and you can see why they do it."

Mark looks at me and shakes his head. "You did a good job of explaining that stuff, bro. Maybe you should become a teacher."

"I think I would enjoy being a teacher. It would be hard, but I have a feeling it could be the perfect fit."

"When you know what you're talking about, you're a great teacher. I'll give you that. Remember when you taught me how to play the guitar. You were so patient, and you never gave up with me even when I was struggling."

"Yeah, I remember. Thanks."

"As for the airlines, now they just need to find a way to be on time more than like 10% of the time."

"Dude, they travel thousands of miles and arrive as scheduled the majority of the time. You can't ever get to my place on time and it's twenty minutes away."

"Shut up, dude."

CHAPTER 6

"A dollar won is twice as sweet as a dollar earned."

—Paul Newman, *The Color of Money*

When I fly to Las Vegas, I always try to get a window seat. There is something truly special about seeing all the lights as you fly into the city. Las Vegas might be the only city in the world that is the product of pure capitalism. I always know deep down that I am going to lose when I visit Las Vegas. I try to stay as confident as possible, but it's to no avail. A trip to Las Vegas is more like a prison sentence that ends when your flight departs at weekend's end. And what crime have the visitors committed? You name it.

The most frustrating part of the fact that I usually lose in Las Vegas is that I consider myself an excellent gambler. I know all the right moves in blackjack, but I never seem to come out ahead. I don't know if I'm unlucky, but given the amount of times that I've been there I should have come out on top more often. I ultimately realized that I needed to play a game that relied at least as much on skill as on luck. This is why I began playing poker.

I started playing poker in my senior year in college while living with six other fraternity brothers. One of my roommates knew I liked to gamble, so he challenged me to a friendly game. We started to play a couple times a week, and within a month all my roommates were getting into the action. There was a game almost every night, and friends and fraternity brothers were soon standing in line to join in. In the end, it was the camaraderie and friendships that I will remember most about those college days. I honestly didn't mind losing $30 if I was hanging out with my friends. It was entertainment to me, and whether I won or lost was for the most part irrelevant. That's not to say that I wasn't a lot happier when I pocketed $50 for the night.

Incredibly, the last time I was in Las Vegas I played poker at the Mirage and won a hefty sum of money. During the first couple of days on this trip, I stuck to the small stakes tables, but once I was up, I decided to test my skills in the high stakes games. It was an enjoyable experience, because not only do I love to play poker and build some confidence, but I also came home a winner. A big winner.

I had never told anyone about that experience, but I figured I could tell my brothers about it over the weekend. We were in Las Vegas after all, and I wanted to play a lot of poker. Besides, if you can't tell your own brothers about these things, you've got a much bigger problem than the Queen of Diamonds.

Mark, Ben and I took a cab to the Mirage, the hotel where we were staying for the weekend. Jon was going to meet us at the hotel. He was flying from out East, and would be arriving a bit later. We all met up in the hotel room and were thrilled to be together. As per the usual, we each anticipated numerous sports conversations and some classic dialogue on other subjects that most people would consider ridiculous. The funny part about our conversations is that they all started with something amazingly mundane, but, by the end, they somehow became deep. Over the course of a weekend, we often talked about our individual lives and the next step in our careers or our relationships. But, there have been just as many times when we would look back and realize we talked about nothing important at all. Sometimes, I guess you just need to have fun and not worry about the daily grind in your life.

We had never gone to Las Vegas together. This trip was a fluke because Ben had won four free tickets to Las Vegas through his company. When one brother would visit another, which was pretty frequent, we usually did nothing special. When most people visit their friends or relatives, they always have to go see something or engage in some significant activity, whether it be taking a tour of Alcatraz or going to a reunion with other relatives. That always seemed to be part of their reason for visiting. As for my brothers and I, seeing each other alone made the journey worthwhile. I wasn't sure what would be in store for this trip, but I had a feeling it would consist mostly of drinking, laughing and gambling. None of us was a real "clubber," and the truth was that during times like this we would all rather just hang out together in our hotel room and do nothing than find ourselves in some crazy scene like a Las Vegas club. Whatever happened, with my brothers around, I knew that it was all good.

CHAPTER 7

"Some people live to eat. I eat to live."

—Socrates

One of the most intriguing aspects of a trip to Las Vegas is how upset someone will become upon losing a couple hundred dollars. That same person might lose thousands of dollars a day on the stock market without giving it a second thought. And these days, the stock market is more of a gamble than the blackjack table. The power of watching your money dwindle in front of your face is an incredible thing. Any casino regular will tell you that this is one of the main reasons casinos use chips; it makes you feel like you aren't losing money, just a few meaningless tokens down the drain in a friendly game with your buddies. Las Vegas is smart, maybe the smartest city in the world.

I find one of the saddest aspects of a trip to Las Vegas to be those people who are so concerned about losing their money that they can't enjoy their time. It's very easy to lose all your money in one hour (well it is for me, anyway, since I have almost no money to begin with). I understand people's frustration; I just wish they didn't let winning or losing determine whether they're happy or sad. I recognize that it will have some impact—I'm not a complete dope—but just don't let yourself lose so much that you want to throw yourself out the nearest window. You can win it back. It's not a college football game, for God's sake.

To make sure that we didn't traverse the ugly path of three-hours-and-your-out, my brothers and I decided to start the evening by heading to some cheap blackjack tables over at the Imperial Palace. After an hour of cards and numerous drinks, we decided to head back to the Mirage to grab some dinner. We headed for the California Pizza Kitchen (CPK), which happens to be right next to the casino. CPK was packed, so it took us about ten minutes to grab a seat. We were having a good time chatting, when I saw something that caught my eye.

Now, what I'm going to expound upon in the next few pages might seem a bit preposterous, but give me a chance to explain. I am going to try to make the argument that a host at a restaurant actually has an important job. All right, no one hosts as a career, but that doesn't diminish its importance, as you shall see.

First, a little background. I had never hosted before last year when I was between jobs, having been laid-off along with everyone else out in San Francisco. I needed some extra income to sustain my expenses while I searched for another job. I figured I would get a waiting job, or hopefully bartend. I knew, however, that as soon as a better job came along, I'd bolt, which left me with a choice when I started applying for actual positions—pretend that I was in for the long run or fess up from the start.

It turned out that I had a friend that used to work for CPK, and I mentioned to her that I was looking for some work. She said she would make a call or two, and the next thing I know I get an email from an HR lady at corporate headquarters saying that I should contact the manager at the nearby CPK in San Francisco. I think that was the only time I've ever benefited from a connection. Some people get a job as an associate with their father-in-law's law firm, or as a CPA with one of the big accounting firms. I get hitched to CPK. Still, at that particular moment, desperate as I was for work, you would've thought I'd struck gold.

I interviewed the following week and immediately told the manager, "I have to be honest from the start, I don't know how long I'm going to be here, but I promise you two weeks." Not a typical introduction to a manager, right? I couldn't believe I was being honest in an interview at a restaurant. Most people I know would claim to be Wolfgang Puck if they were interviewing for a stupid line-cook position, but I had to be honest, not only for myself, but because I didn't want to lose the trust of my friend. You've seen *Donnie Brasco*, right? She vouched for me. I couldn't let her down.

By the end of the interview, I could tell the manager liked me, and I thought he was very nice. I'm sure I don't have to tell you that an excellent manager at a restaurant, and in fact anywhere, is crucial to the success of an organization. Turnover is very high in the restaurant industry, but employees will stick around much longer than they otherwise would if they like their manager. This is obviously big. Less turnover equals less training equals more efficiency, meaning more money.

When the interview was over, the manager told me he would be right back after speaking with the assistant manager for a moment. When he returned, he said, "Well, it's not worth training you for a waiter position, but we do need a host. It's eight bucks per hour, plus tips, and you get a free meal. What do you think?" I was thrilled. I took the job and became a host for the first time in my life.

Now, back to why hosting is actually an important job, and the events that caught my eye as we were eating our dinner. While grabbing the last slice of my Barbecue Chicken Pizza, a CPK classic, I had an opportunity to watch a scene unfold around the host area of the restaurant. The restaurant was just coming down from about an hour of heavy traffic. Although all the tables still had customers, an observant host would have been able to tell that many customers were about to finish their meals and pay their checks.

An older lady walked up to that stand in front of the door—you know, the one with the seating chart and the reservation book—and began craning her neck in search of the host. At that particular moment, the host was in the kitchen, putting away some dishes after clearing a few tables. Our waiter, who was extremely busy and hard at work, greeted the new patron at the host stand. She asked my waiter how long the wait would be for a party of four. The waiter looked around, and said, "Now? We're really busy. At least a half-hour." The lady was disappointed, and actually a little surprised. After a moment's hesitation, she wheeled around and headed out of the Mirage to presumably grab some food with her friends at another restaurant.

The point here is this. The waiter had no clue about the flow of the restaurant at that moment in time. He could probably have only told you the status of his own tables, a small percentage of the entire restaurant, and rightly his primary concern. Still, within 15 minutes, three tables had opened and were left unfilled because there were no new customers. Nevertheless, it wasn't the waiter's responsibility to fill those tables, and frankly he never should have thrust himself into that role. The poor sap was in way above his head. Although he was trying to help by greeting the customer, he ended up doing more harm than good. The waiter cost the restaurant an opportunity to earn more revenue. Since the vacated tables stayed empty at least while we were there, when at least one could have been filled, the restaurant didn't get the revenue it would have brought in if only the potential customer had been greeted by the host.

If it doesn't seem like a big deal for a waiter to miscalculate the wait for a restaurant, let's do a little math. I would guess that the average meal per person at a CPK is $15. For argument's sake, let's assume the potential table would have been a party of four. If so, the restaurant lost $60 because of the waiter's well-intended, but foolhardy mistake. And the reality is that this type of thing happens all the time. Even hosts don't provide accurate predictions of how long the wait will be at a restaurant. That is exactly why an excellent host can make such a big difference to the bottom line of a busy restaurant. If a host's miscalculation needlessly causes two groups to leave a restaurant each day, and the tables do not go filled, that could easily cost the restaurant $120 a day in lost revenue. Over the year, that amounts to over a whopping sum of $40,000 down the drain. Admit it, its mind-boggling to think that a host at a busy restaurant could be that important to the bottom line.

What does all this mean? If you will allow me to moralize for a moment (this is the self-help part of the book where I try to make a difference and strike a blow for the little guy), it means that we should stop blowing off hosts as "mindless" gatekeepers of a restaurant, and rather treat them as people with a reasonable amount of responsibility who are doing an important job for a restaurant. In other words, every employee counts. If you don't value all your employees, co-workers or whomever, well then, my friend, you're missing out on the bottom line as well.

CHAPTER 8

"Not everything that can be counted counts, and not every-thing that counts can be counted."

—Albert Einstein

After dinner, we headed back to the hotel room to get ready for the night. We figured we would rest for a little while, maybe watch a sports game on television, and then get back to the action at some casino. I walked into the room first, and knowing that my brothers would do the same thing, I quickly grabbed the remote control from the nightstand to turn on the television. As I'm sure you know, possession of the remote control brings with it a certain amount of power, and power can be a very dangerous thing.

I would compare the remote control to the Ring in the *Lord of the Rings*. He who has the remote has unspeakable power, but how will the bearer choose to use it? Will he be able to withstand the evil tendencies that come with having the remote and choose programming that is suitable to all? Or will the holder of the remote succumb to its powers, and selfishly pursue stimulation solely of his own audio and visual needs, to hell with all the others? In the *Lord of the Rings*, as we all know, Middle Earth was very lucky that the Ring fell into Bilbo's hands. Bilbo, like most hobbits, was far more concerned about living comfortably and having fun, than he was desirous of gaining any power. He and Frodo, his nephew, were each chosen by fate to accomplish a task that neither wanted to undertake. Though small and meek, it was these diminutive qualities that ultimately made the hobbits uniquely capable of destroying the Ring. In the end, the evil powers of the Ring were not strong enough to alter the fundamental qualities and values of these hobbits.

However, the Ring did manage to dominate and manipulate otherwise "good," but weak-minded individuals such as the human warrior, Boromir. Boromir, a member of the Fellowship, demonstrated by his eventual attack on Frodo that he lacked the integrity, honesty, wisdom and skill to handle the power of the Ring. His mind and spirit were too weak to contain an object of such power. I know many Boromir-like individuals who prove similarly unwise and weak-willed before the fierce face of the remote control. Someone like Boromir would use a remote control to satisfy his own visual needs, lacking any true sense of how to even-handedly handle this powerful object. He would simply be incapable of managing a remote on behalf of a group, a fellowship if you may. He would be the kind of guy who demonstrates basic remote surfing inadequacies. Boromir would easily have missed critical television programming—the critical result on a score ticker, the crucial seconds of every show that immediately follow a commercial, or a classic movie moment. After a certain amount of time, his companions would realize he is not worthy of the remote, and they would become angry and discontent. A fight to gain control of the remote would ensue, and in the end, no one would really win.

Now the opposite of Boromir would be, Gandalf the prototypical wizard. Gandalf was too wise to accept the Ring from Bilbo. Gandalf realized that there would be extremely dangerous implications should someone with his vast knowledge and powers wield the Ring. The Ring was so potent that, in spite of himself, Gandalf would not have been able to help but abuse its powers to his own end, leading irrevocably, albeit unwittingly, to a reign of terror of catastrophic proportions for the denizens of Middle Earth. Gandalf, an introspective soul, clearly realized that it would be far worse for the Ring to fall into his hands than it would were it to end up with Boromir, who would certainly court a degree of disaster but would be incapable of wreaking anywhere near the same kind of havoc. If Gandalf had the remote control, he would watch some niche network like the History Channel, even though most "common-folk" could care less about that type of programming. He would become so warped by the powerful forces of the remote control that he would become incapable of effectively listening to his companion's television needs. It is not that he didn't have the proper skills to manage the remote effectively; he would just believe himself rightly compelled to choose something that only he considered interesting. In turn, while Boromir would royally screw things up, at least we'd get to basically watch what we wanted to. With Gandalf at the helm, we would miss out on essential programming in its entirety. This is a horror that clearly cannot be permitted. Of course, in reality this would be moot since Gandalf would probably rather read than waste his time watching television! Nevertheless...

I guess the main point of all this *Lord of the Ring* talk is to demonstrate that when I'm with my brothers, we recognize the necessity of becoming hobbits. Each of us harmoniously realizes that it's more important to be Frodo or Bilbo, and perhaps appear weak to an outsider, than it is to be Gandalf, and appear too strong. Admittedly, every one of us has, at times, proven wizard-like in our ambition, and at other times so foolhardy and misdirected as to give Boromir a run for his money, but far more often we display the heart of a hobbit. Perhaps, like these inhabitants of the Shire who were able to coexist peacefully while chaos reigned all around them, this is why my brothers and I have managed to peacefully coexist for so many years before the power of the remote.

Luckily, we are all huge sports fans, and any true sports fan usually does the same thing when they turn on the tube. If you're trying to decide, think about what you do when you turn on the television: Do you start with ESPN, ESPN2, and if there is some major story, ESPNews? If you want to watch a highlight yet again, do you quickly check FoxSports or CNNSI? When there is a big sports game on television, do all questions as to where to look first become moot, since you naturally first flip to the game to check the score, and then while at commercial revert to more traditional channel surfing? During baseball season, do you immediately check the ticker for scores upon turning on the tube? And if ESPN is at commercial do you go to Headline News for score updates as well?

Do you feel teased by Headline News because their ticker is so slow? Do you know the pain of waiting through an entire ticker, the exhilaration of knowing your game is next up, and then the stab of agony when the program cuts out to commercial just before the pivotal score arrives? Have you, like me, experienced many an anxious minute, waiting to see your team's score on the small ticker? Have you come to discover that, similar to the adrenaline rush of doubling down in blackjack and seeing what card you get, the little ticker can rack you with nervousness, elevate you in happiness, level you with despair or shock you with disbelief? God help me, am I really talking about a freaking ticker?

One of the beauties of sports is that everyone can usually agree to watch the same game on television. In sports, no one knows the ending. When it comes to movies, on the other hand, everyone seems to be of different mindsets. So back in the hotel with my brothers, as I was flipping through the channels, I found myself in a quandary: a movie or a sporting event. I opted for ESPN Classic. The channel that shows the best sporting events of all time. The channel that magically transforms a sports game into a classic movie where we all know the final score and the drama we experienced when we witnessed the event live. The channel that, when you are with friends or brothers, inevitably generates some debate, or at the very least leads to an interesting conversation.

And, of course, that is what happened when I was with my brothers in the hotel room, watching ESPN Classic. I can't remember the exact game, but it was one of the classic Yankee comebacks during their dynasty run in the late 1990's.

Derek Jeter, base hit.

MARK: Jeter is incredible.

JON: The guy makes more clutch hits and plays than anyone else I've ever seen.

MIKE: I'll never like the Yankees, but I must say that they were the clutchest bunch of players I've ever seen. They all seemed to have the ability to get the big hit. It didn't matter if they had gone 0 for their last 14. If it was late in the game, everyone knew that somehow they were going to get the win.

BEN: Intangibles. All their players had intangibles. Look at their roster. There was no superstar that completely stood out like a Bonds or a Sosa. Jeter epitomizes intangibles. The guy doesn't hit home runs. The guy doesn't get 150 RBIs. Yet, we all know that he's the leader that made that team click.

JON: Yeah, you're right. Take a player like Gary Sheffield, that guy has zero intangibles. He brings a team down despite his unbelievable statistics. He's the polar opposite of a guy like Svoboda in Genesis NHL Hockey '94!

I feel compelled to point out that my brother just referred to an animated hockey player as a "guy." That's funny.

MIKE: The greatest video game ever created! And I am still the best ever, despite my one freak loss to you courtesy of Svoboda. You always find a way to bring that up. So my record against you is 99-1. Big deal.

MARK: Who the hell is Svoboda?

JON: Dude, don't ever say Svoboda wasn't a big deal. He had you in misery for months. Admit it, you're still traumatized by all my gloating and your three months of shame? Granted, after the 90 days that I refused to play you in order to keep my "streak" alive, you ran off 73 straight games, but Svoboda gave me a full quarter of a year of fame and glory.

BEN: Who was he?

JON: Svoboda was this defender on Buffalo who had a rating of like 50 out of 100. He was super slow. I was playing Mike in a classic confrontation, during Mike's prime in '94 and '95. With thirty seconds left in the third period, and the score deadlocked at two, I took Svoboda coast to coast. The funny thing about it was that he wouldn't go down. No matter how many times Mike body-checked him, the guy refused to be stopped. We watched it on instant replay like three times, well I did, and he was hit six times before he scored. All I can say is that the little dude had the will and drive to succeed. Svoboda epitomized intangibles. The guy didn't put up the numbers, but he was a winner.

BEN: They should create a category on sports video games for intangibles. Like Jeter would have a 97 intangible rating, and someone like Sheffield would have a 30.

MARK: Dude, that would be sweet. But isn't the whole point of intangibles that they can't be measured?

MIKE: Yet, if I gave a list of 15 players, I bet we would put them all in the same order for level in terms of their intangibles.

JON: Jordan's intangible would be ridiculous. He might set the standard.

MIKE: Intangibles are just like Quality. You can't measure Quality, yet we all know what separates something that is Quality from something that sucks.

MARK: Where have I heard that before?

JON: Sounds familiar…

MIKE: I made that up myself…. What? All right, fine. I stole it from that damn book you made me read, *Zen and The Art of Motorcycle Maintenance.*

BEN: Zen what? What are you guys talking about?

JON: Dude, get with it. It's a classic American novel. It's the book Phil Jackson made Scottie Pippen read.

BEN: Oh…. You know I don't like to read.

MARK: Mike, you're right. Intangibles are just like Quality.

BEN: Yet, day in and day out society seems to prefer players and employees who have the big numbers but don't have the intangibles.

JON: It is sad. But the problem is that intangibles aren't seen after just one day. Intangibles take time to notice, while numbers are easy to understand from the start. If we were playing in a basketball game where I came off the bench and scored the next 15 points to tie the game, you would think I absolutely made the difference.

MARK: Are we talking about real life or make believe, 'cause you've never scored 15 points in a real game.

JON: Whatever. But what if I came off the bench and didn't score, and we still tied the game? You might hypothesize that I was the reason for the comeback after a little while, but you wouldn't know for sure like you would if I had scored all 15 points. Statistics help us escape from making difficult decisions based on subjectivity. A knowledgeable sports fan may have seen that I was responsible for the difference. But someone who never plays would assume that I was just helping the team's cause, not that I was the main factor in the comeback. They probably wouldn't even recognize that we made the run only after I came on the court.

MIKE: What we know for a fact we understand. No one can ever prove that you were the difference in the game, but someone can prove that your teammate scored 15 points. That's why everyone would assume your teammate was the star. But was he the difference?

BEN: That type of shit happens to me every day at work. I'm sick of being the man "behind-the-scenes." I do all the work for this presentation, and then my manager shows it to upper-management and gets all the credit. He barely even mentions my name in the report. I do all the work, all the research, all the editing, and he gets all the credit. The business world is such bullshit. It's killing me. I wish they could have a box score in the business world.

MARK: But your box score wouldn't be that good. That's the whole point, bro. You're worth more than a box score. A box score just summarizes a game, it doesn't tell you the whole story. Have you ever seen a box score for some of Jason Kidd's games? He shoots 1 for 10, has 5 assists, and grabs 6 rebounds. It doesn't seem like he played a good game, right? Then you ask all the players who was the MVP of the game and all of them say Kidd. And you know they're right. The box score means nothing to him and to his game. His contribution goes beyond a box score. A box score actually makes Kidd's game look worse at times. Yet, we all agree he's the best point guard in the league. He has all the intangibles that are needed to succeed. You have them too, Ben. You've just gotta keep working hard, bro. You'll get yours.

BEN: I'm like the #2 batter in a baseball lineup. I do all the work and everyone else gets the credit. Just once I'd like to be the guy cleaning up and smacking homers.

JON: That's not your style though. You don't hit homers. You play smart ball, get base hits, and advance runners. You do all the little things that a team needs to get in order to win, but you totally get overshadowed. You are a #2 batter.

MIKE: Why do guys say that the #2 batter doesn't get any credit? There are plenty of good #2 hitters.

JON: Okay. Name me three lead-off hitters and three sluggers. Then name me three #2 batters.

MIKE: Fine. Ichiro. Damon. Lofton. Giambi. Bonds. Ramirez. Jeter…umm…umm…

JON: Not that easy is it. #2 hitters do not get their due. To be honest, though, they probably aren't as good as hitters either.

MIKE: But they are in one of the worst positions to put up big numbers. You don't want to be at the #2 spot if you're trying to pad your statistics. Maybe that's why we think Jeter has so many intangibles.... The truth is he has intangibles on top of the fact that he sits in a position that isn't known for putting up big numbers.

BEN: I've got it!

MARK: What?

MIKE: Oh Jesus.

JON: What man?

BEN: The RCI.

MIKE: Dude, that's RBI, Runs Batted In. Are you stoned?

JON: You didn't honestly refer to the RBI as RCI?

BEN: Will you guys shut up for a second? I got something here. Hear me out. I can explain it better with an example. The leadoff hitter gets a base hit. The #2 man gets a single, and the leadoff hitter goes to third. The #3 batter strikes out. Then #4 gets a single to bring in the leadoff hitter. The #5 and #6 hitters strike out to end the inning. Now, lets go over the statistics. The #1 batters gets a hit and a run. The #4 player gets a hit and an RBI. The #2 hitter only gets a hit. Why do we give someone credit for bringing a player home with an RBI, but don't have any statistic for getting someone in scoring position? Wasn't the #2 batter's hit just as valuable to that run? It was crucial. Plus, it's a lot easier to hit with a guy on third, than it is to hit with a guy on first. I think I just invented a new baseball statistic! The RCI. Runs Contributed In.

JON: Actually, that's a fuckin' good point. Although we do have the sacrifice. Being able to sacrifice is important for a #2 batter. That's a big part of their job description.

BEN: The RCI incorporates the sacrifice. A player receives an RCI anytime that he advances a runner and that same runner scores as a result. He also gets an RCI if he scores since you obviously contribute to your own run. The most RCIs you can get per at-bat is four. In the example I gave before, #1 would get an RCI, #2 would get an RCI, and #4 would get an RCI.

MARK: It seems like there would be too many RCIs. It would be too high a number.

JON: I don't know. I actually think it might be a better gauge of how much a player does for the team. An RBI only tells you something about the guys who happen to be at-bat when a run actually scores. An RCI tells you something about the contribution made by all the players who are on base or maybe even no longer on base when a run is produced. It's a more thorough statistic.

MIKE: It's like an assist in basketball or hockey. That's what a #2 batter is anyway, an assist man to help the #3 and #4 drive in the runs. Assists are sometimes the main reason for a goal, right?

MARK: I still think there would be too many RCIs. Everybody would be getting credit for a run.

BEN: That's the whole point. It's a team game, dude. They were all equally responsible for the run in my eyes. All players involved should get some statistic saying they were part of it. They all played a big role in the run.

MIKE: Mark, if you were a supporting actor in a movie, you would still want to be in the credits, right?

MARK: Yeah, but the star should be first.

MIKE: But the star isn't necessarily the reason the movie is successful. A supporting actor can be the difference in the success or failure of a movie, even if he is in only one or two scenes. Take *A Few Good Men* for example. Nicholson made the movie, even though he was only in the movie for about 30 minutes, if that. Shouldn't Jack get just as much credit for the success of the movie as Demi Moore or Tom Cruise? I think he should. I'm not taking anything away from Cruise, he deserves his share of acclaim as well, it's just they both helped to make the movie a hit. It wasn't just one individual.

JON: So what would be considered a good year for RCIs?

BEN: Well, for every run and RBI you get, you would get an RCI, so it would have to be over 200 for the best players. Another thing, if you hit a homer, you only get one RCI for yourself. You don't add the run and the RBI. My guess would be that a 400 RCI year would lead the league. We should tape like 80 games for one team next year and follow their RCI totals. That way we could project the totals for the season.

JON: It is amazing that they've never thought about a statistic like that before. In all these years, they've only referred to the advancing of a runner as a "sacrifice," if anything at all. It was as if it was just an honorable thing to do. Yet today, here in this hotel room, we have revolutionized the game of baseball forever. No longer is moving a runner just an act of valor, but something integral to the end result of the game. It's an offensive statistic that should show up in the box score.

MIKE: Don't get all sensitive on us, Jon. We know you love the game, but it's only an RCI, a close cousin of the RBI.... But wait! What happens if there's an error? I get on first, moving the runner to second because of an error. Then the next guy drives in the run. Do I get an RCI? The other guy definitely gets an RBI and an RCI, and the guy who comes in gets an RCI and a run. But what about the guy who got on because of the error?

BEN: I'd say no. You should only get an RCI if you advance the runner without an error. If you get out and move the runner to second without an error, then yes, you should get an RCI. Sure, it's probably not the way you wanted it to happen, but you still did enough to get the guy into scoring position. You could have easily struck out or hit into a double play. Even if it wasn't much, you still did something to contribute to the run. Ergo, the RCI.

JON: What about if I'm batting and I get on first because of an error, but I ultimately score?

BEN: In that case, I would say you would still get an RCI. You always contribute to your own run, even if you did not really earn it. You still had to make your way from first to home, after all. I'm gonna write this stuff down. I'm sure there are a million scenarios that we could come up with to test the credibility of the statistic, but for right now, I'll just start with the basics. I could have possibly just come up with the most important baseball statistic ever. I am the Einstein of baseball statistics. The Commissioner will be hearing about this, baby!

JON: Dude, you're not even the Einstein of bagels…. Are you seriously going to send the new statistic to the Commissioner? You should. Wouldn't it be awesome if he actually responds?

BEN: We'll have to work out the finer details, such as whether or not guys who advance runners should get an RCI if a batter hits a home run. But after I watch about 80 games, I should have a good sense of how accurate and effective the stat can be. By July, the Commissioner will have my memo on his desk and an essay explaining why the everyday box score should include a new category known as the RCI.

MARK: But you're forgetting the whole point of what got us going to begin with, Ben. The box score doesn't tell the whole story. A man should be more than just his statistics. Character and leadership are just as important for the team, if not more important. You're better than a box score, even if you can't find some way to quantify the fact that you're basically the #2 batter in your job.

BEN: Well, I think it's about time we find a way to give someone like me a little more credit. If this is the way I have to do it, then so be it.

MARK: True, true. I hear you brother. Let's shower up and get back down to the casino. I need a few more beers in my belly.

SATURDAY

CHAPTER 9

"Twenty years from now you will be more disappointed by the things you didn't do than by the ones you did do. So throw off the bowlines. Sail away from the safe harbour. Catch the trade winds in your sails. Explore. Dream. Discover."

—Mark Twain

We ended up partying down at the Hard Rock Casino until four in the morning. None of us came out ahead, but none of us lost more than $50, so we all felt good about ourselves. One run in blackjack and we would all have our money back.

It was already getting late in the morning. Jon and I decided to head down the strip over to the Bellagio. I wanted to check out the poker room, and Jon had never been there before. Mark and Ben decided that they wanted to get a few more hours of sleep.

On the walk to the Bellagio, I figured this might be a good time to mention something to my brother about my poker experience the last time I was in Las Vegas. I always find it a lot easier to talk about an important issue with just one person, as opposed to a group of people. It's tough to process advice when three people are expressing their opinions all at once. When I seek out a person for advice, I go to someone who I know can handle the fact that I might not follow his or her suggestions. Most people seem to take it personally if someone doesn't follow their path of advice. It's not that I don't value other people's opinions or input, it's just that I may end up choosing another route. In this regard, I always found Jon to be a great person to talk to about important decisions. He has the capacity to see that it isn't between him and me, but between my life and me. I know Jon wants to help me, and I know he knows I want his help. I respect his opinion, and I wanted to hear what he had to say about this poker thing. After a few minutes discussing the amount of alcohol we all consumed the night before, I finally gathered the internal fortitude to talk about my more pressing concerns.

MIKE: Jon, you're not going to believe what happened to me the last time I was out here.

JON: Didn't we already go over this? Three prostitutes in your hotel room. Didn't I tell you to never bring more than one prostitute back at a time! Just a waste of cash.

MIKE: Funny, but no. Not into that stuff anymore…

JON: What happened then?

MIKE: The last time I was here I played some poker and won a couple grand.

JON: Are you serious?

MIKE: Yeah.

JON: That's awesome. That's a lot of cash. Why didn't you tell anyone?

MIKE: I don't know. Just figured when you win that type of cash you should keep it to yourself.

JON: Yeah, probably a smart move. How did you win so much money? Were you playing big stakes games?

MIKE: I started at the small tables and won a decent sum, so I decided to step it up a notch and play off my profit in the bigger games. If I went back to even, I figured I would stop. I never had to.

JON: That's incredible. You must've gone on a major lucky streak.

MIKE: Give me some credit. You know how I started playing cards with my buddies when I was in college.

JON: Yeah, but everyone does that, and everyone doesn't win a few grand in Vegas.

MIKE: I've been reading a lot of poker books lately, and when I get a chance I like to go to the local casinos and play a little.

JON: You read poker books? Poker has books?

MIKE: You wouldn't believe how many books there are on poker. It's a seriously tough game, and it's not just about being smart mathematically. To really win, you've gotta be able to read players and understand the essence of the game. This takes some Jeter-like intangibles. You got it or you don't.

JON: Have the books helped you?

MIKE: You wouldn't believe how much. In retrospect, these books have been like an investment. And, trust me, they've paid off. If I play only one hand better because of that book, it's already a profitable investment. Still, reading a few books won't make you good at cards. Poker's a streets-smart game, which is why I like it.

JON: You should do something with that money. Maybe have some fun with it. I know you're miserable at work. If you end up getting laid-off, you should do something cool. Maybe you could go away for a while. Do a bit more traveling. Go somewhere totally different.

MIKE: I've thought about what I would do with the cash, but I need more money than that to just go away.

JON: True, but maybe you're on to something here. You know, I've been telling you to find a way to take a break and do something different, something that would have meaning to you. Maybe poker could be your big break. I don't know…who does? Who's to say how you make your money. If you don't do stuff while you're young, you'll never do them while you're old. You have the rest of your life to work, bro. You owe no money and have no "true" responsibilities yet, except to yourself. Maybe you need to make a change.

MIKE: What are you saying, Jon?

JON: You need to get that pep back that you used to have. I think you would get a lot out of taking a break and really thinking about what you want to do for the next few years. What you're doing now isn't working. There's nothing wrong with that. It happened to me. It happens to a lot of people. I think you should go away, travel or something. Maybe if you give yourself a little space, you'll find your calling along the way. Maybe not, but you would still at the very least end up with an incredible experience that you'd never forget. Nothing really changes back home. Work is always work.

MIKE: How much money do you think I'd need?

JON: Let's say you decide to go away for five or six months. I would guess that you'd probably need about six grand to cover all your expenses, including the flight.

MIKE: I don't know. I have almost nothing in savings, and I can't save a dime in San Francisco because it's so expensive out there. I'm not going anywhere, anytime soon.

JON: Well, like I said, maybe something will turn up.

MIKE: Where would I even go? I wouldn't mind going back to Europe.

JON: If I were you, I wouldn't just go to Europe again. You'll be there over and over again throughout your life. In the scheme of things, Europe isn't so different from America. Do something that will totally expand your mind, Mike. See totally different cultures. Take a lot of time and go somewhere really out there, like India or South East Asia.

MIKE: Asia? Travel for six months?

JON: What? You thought a two-week vacation would do the trick? Trust me bro, after all the crap with your jaw and the shitty jobs you've had out here, you need the trip of all trips. Think about it. You're not going away tomorrow. It'll take you a bit of time to save that much money. The more I think about it, the more I know I'm right. When you finally have enough money to travel, get moving before your life flashes away.

MIKE: I'll definitely mull it over. Sounds like a halfway decent plan.

JON: Actually, changing gears a little bit, I've always wanted to play some poker, but I know I'll look like a beginner and end up getting burned.

MIKE: You know that I enjoy nothing more than teaching my older brother a lesson or two. Listen up for 15 minutes, and then play with me for a few hours. We'll have a blast!

CHAPTER 10

"I'm a poker player. Some might call me a gambler, but I draw a distinction. A gambler plays when the odds are immutable and against him. I don't. That's why there is a large coterie of professional poker players, but not a single, solitary, professional roulette or craps player. In poker, good players win and poor players lose."

—Lou Krieger

After walking around the casino for a while, Jon decided that he would play poker with me. He wanted to find out how good I really was at this, the card game of all card games, and determine once and for all whether poker truly is a game of luck or skill. That, of course, is the eternal question in poker. Many relationships have ended because the two sides were unable to compromise on an answer. To me, the truth is clear. Words of advice: if there is any question in your mind as to what poker's really about, watch *Rounders,* one of the best movies around.

JON: Hey Mike, let's grab a drink at that sports bar while you tell me what I need to know before we play. Win or lose, if I can come away without looking like a total beginner, I'll be happy.

MIKE: I'm pretty sure I can help you reach that goal. What games do you know?

JON: I know 7-Card Stud and a couple of other games, but I know playing at a casino is a whole different ballgame.

MIKE: Relax bro. You're going to be fine. 7-Card Stud is my game of choice.

JON: Cool.

MIKE: Okay, the first thing you need to know is that poker is a microcosm of life. Like life, poker isn't really about luck. In fact, I'd go so far as to say that it's actually a complete skill game, with just a drop of luck involved to keep it interesting for all. When you sit at a table, you're going to be playing against great players and bad players. You're going to be playing against sharks and old ladies. You'll be up against drunks and cowboys. The point is that, also like life, no matter who sits across from you, you still have to play your game. Be true to yourself.

JON: But the people you're playing against have to factor into the game you play, right? How much does it matter who you play against?

MIKE: It means tons. The quicker you can figure people out, the better player you will be. It's just really important to play your style of poker. Some people like to take a lot of chances while others are very conservative. The more you play, the more you'll become comfortable with the kind of player you are. I'm not saying that your game isn't impacted by who sits at your table, just that you don't want to get duped into playing to someone else's game. Like if someone is betting hard, and you're not really a hard better, you shouldn't become one just because this guy is throwing down a lot of cash. You'll end up playing right into their hands. The quickest way to lose is to fail to be consistent to your own style and personality.

JON: I think I'm following you, but I need more specifics.

MIKE: Since we don't know enough to know what kind of player you are, I'm going to show you how I play. You might end up tweaking it here or there, but long-term, I think the way I play will give you the best chance of winning on a regular basis.

JON: All right, I'm all ears.

MIKE: Okay. Let me ask you a question. Do you consider where you are today luck? Was it luck that you got good grades in school?

JON: There were definitely some things that were out of my control, but I studied my ass off in school, so I'd say no, more skill than luck.

MIKE: Right. And when you boil it down, school is a game just like poker. In school, the other students are your competition. And like any class in school, poker involves some study if you want to consistently beat your competition. You can't just play poker and win consistently. You have to study the game, but in poker the studying takes place while on-the-job. Luck can only get you so far, and it's not very far at all in poker.

JON: Okay, okay. Poker isn't about luck. I got it.

MIKE: The most important rule in poker is that the more patient you are, the better chance you will have to win. I repeat, if you aren't patient, you will not win in poker. You shouldn't even bother to play. It really is that simple. So, two things so far: don't rely on luck and be patient.

JON: I wouldn't call patience one of your greatest virtues.

MIKE: I agree. But when it comes to poker I'm a totally different person. Luckily, I had someone tell me early on that patience was the key. Otherwise, I would have found out the hard way. Patience in poker basically means folding every time on the shoot, the initial deal, until you have a good hand to play.

JON: Folding? That means you lost the hand.

MIKE: No! That's what everyone thinks, but it's not true. You don't usually ante when you play at the casino. And even if you do, the ante is such a small amount that it's not worth playing for when you have a bad hand. Folding isn't a bad thing. It's often the smartest thing you can do, and it's usually free. You can sit at a poker table, fold for an hour straight, get free drinks from the hot cocktail waitresses and no one will care. The best part for you is that most people don't even follow this rule. The majority of gamblers for one reason or another are typically not patient enough to let the game come to them. It's like they forget that they don't have to bet if they've got nothing to bet on. The bottom line is that when you do have a good hand, there's a pretty decent chance that some of the other people betting have garbage. Not that you should count on it, but it ends up being true.

JON: Really?

MIKE: Yep. The other funny part about folding all the time is that the other players will actually think you're a good player! They'll presume that you're so disciplined, so cool and calculating, that when you do play a hand, they feel compelled to show you respect. And, sometimes, all you really wanted were some free drinks!

JON: Folding every time sounds sort of boring. I want to play the game, not watch it.

MIKE: Sitting at a desk and staring at a computer is boring. Folding gives you time to evaluate your competition, which is often more important than the cards you hold. When you fold a hand you're only out of that one battle. It doesn't mean you've lost the war. To win the war, you have to study your opponents. Which players play every hand? Which players are winning the pots? How does this person bet? Does he bet hard early and then get conservative? Or is it the reverse? What were his hidden cards? Does he start with good hands, or did he play the hand only because he got himself too deeply invested? Which players go to the river card, the last card, and then fold? Which players fold every time? These are just some of the questions you need to answer. The quicker you can analyze your competition, the better you'll be. It's like a lion that sits out in the grass all day studying and analyzing his prey. The lion doesn't go after the strongest or fastest animal; it isn't worth his time or energy. The lion goes after the young, sick, or slow animals. In poker, a good player should do the same thing. You should be aggressive against weaker players, and conservative against stronger players. And don't presume that the game gets harder when a bad player gets up to leave. The reality is that there are bound to be weak prey in every field. If you're patient enough, you'll find that player. And if you wait for your opportunity, bidding your time, you'll score big. Most people win money in poker not because they made a smart play, but because their competition made a bad play.

JON: But Mike, if I fold almost every time, won't the other players know that I have a good hand when I finally start betting? I mean, as soon as I start putting money down, won't they just fold?

MIKE: You would think that they would, but people are usually so egocentric that they only consider what they have in their hand and not what you have in your hand. That's why the next rule of poker is that only idiots play a bluffer's game. Sure, you need to change it up every once in a while, but if you're there to bluff, you might as well not even sit down. If you're playing a hand that you think you're losing, and you think the only way for you to win is to bluff the other guy out, then you've already lost. Most people who are in for the long haul don't stay around if they have nothing in their hand. They only stay in the game when they think they have a good hand. Then, there you are, trying to bluff someone out who has a good hand. Big mistake. Would you run a race for money and then give the other guy a head start?

JON: Obviously, no. And in running, the only thing that matters is how you finish. I would assume that's the same in cards.

MIKE: Wrong. Poker is all about how the race is run and often has little to do with the finish. In cards, it's better to be a fast sprinter than it is to be a strong closer. If you don't have the cards to start the game, then you shouldn't be in the game in the first place. A strong closer is a guy who was losing the hand the whole game, and then on the last card he gets lucky and wins the game. They rely on luck more than skill. They may win a hand or even come away big after a night of gambling, but they lose in the long run. The leader sets the pace and tone of a race. If you're trailing, you're forced to run his type of race, keep up with his betting style, etc. In poker, it's very hard to comeback when you fall behind. It takes too much skill and luck. Not only that, the leader could be pacing himself, keeping you close, knowing all along that he can just sprint away when you get to the end of the hand. What I mean is that he might be betting lower than he otherwise might just to keep you hoping, and more importantly betting, when he knows that there's pretty much no way that you can take the hand. That way he suckers you into wasting money to stay in the game, when he knew from the start that he was going to take the pot.

JON: I get the picture, but you're cracking me up. You've managed to compare poker to lions on the prowl, school, and running in races. I'll definitely give you props for oratorical style, but don't you think your pushing it a little bit far. It's freaking cards, dude.

MIKE: There is a lot more to this game than you think, bro. Anyone can play poker; very few can be great at it. You'd be surprised if you read the profiles of the players that win all the big tournaments. Many of those guys have incredible resumes. They would blow your resume away.

JON: Whatever. All right, what's the next thing I need to know, and then let's go play a little. I'm getting tired.

MIKE: Sounds good. Back to the running analogy. If you're going to bet on yourself in a race, you would only bet if you thought you had a good chance to win the race, true?

JON: Yeah, I wouldn't bet if I'm most likely going to lose. It's like when I play you in basketball one-on-one. I would bet on myself every time because I know there's no way I won't beat your ass.

MIKE: You keep on believing that...but I see that you're ready for my next rule. If you're going to the river card, you better be sure you have a damned good chance of winning the hand. If you're just chasing cards, you never should have gone that far to start. To put it another way, you should never be at the river card unless you truly believe you're ahead after the sixth card. In poker, there is no half-way. You get nothing for second place or last place. Actually, being second place is worse than last place. You lost more money. That's why you better be sure that you're going to win the hand if you're going to the end. That's also why you should fold as much as you have to, unless you've got money to burn. And you don't, I've seen your school loan statements!

We entered the poker hall and I asked the manager if there were any spots in $1-$5 Stud. He said that it would be a few minutes, so we waited around the front area until he called our names over the microphone.

MIKE: We're going to play 7-Card Stud. I want you to fold your first five hands so that you can get an idea for the game at a casino, unless, of course, you got aces or some killer hand to start. Most people in the world of poker play Texas Hold'em. In Hold'em, less is known from the start, so you're mostly betting the people. You're playing the players, not the cards. A person who likes Hold'em over Stud proba-bly likes the thrill of the unknown a little bit more. In Stud, you have a much better idea if you should be in the hand or not after the deal. It's much easier for a novice to play. In Stud, you start with three cards out of a total of seven, so 42% of your hand is a known quan-tity before you have to make any decision. There isn't that much more room to improve your hand if you don't start with something good. If 42% of my hand is junk already, why would I play the hand? Still, like I said, most people play bad hands. You just wait and see. It's amazing. Now, in Hold'em, the same rules apply, but you only start with two cards, or 28% of your hand. There is less to bet on in your hand at first. It makes the game a little bit trickier. The game can swing a lot more in Hold'em than in Stud. That's one reason why people love Hold'em so much more.
JON: I think the guy is telling us there are two spots at the table. We

should grab our seats.

MIKE: Remember, be conservative...but play your own game.

We ended up playing for a couple of hours, and Jon had a blast. At one point, he did get burned pretty badly. Jon had a flush and another player pulled a full house. Overall, though, he played a solid game, and even won $5. Most people don't win their first time playing poker at a casino.

JON: How did you end up Mike?

MIKE: I won $60. Not bad for $1-$5 Stud. It's very difficult to come home with a lot of money in that game.

JON: I can't believe I got burned on that flush hand. What were you thinking on that hand?

MIKE: Well, you got unlucky and lucky at the same time. You pulled the flush, and he pulled the full house. He was ahead the whole time, though. You never should have re-raised him. You were so excited about what you had that you didn't stop to think about what he had. It's going to happen. I've done it before. That's poker, though. Poker isn't necessarily about what you hold in your hand. It's about what your opponent has compared to what you have. If you have two pair, you want him to have one pair or a lower two pair; if you have three of a kind, you want him to have two pair. If you have a flush, you want him to have a straight. And if you have a full house, you want him to have a flush. That, unfortunately, is what happened to you. If you're going to win a lot of money, you need to be just one better. If you have a full house and the other players have crap, they'll fold and you won't win a dime.

JON: What do you think was my weakest point? Pick out the thing I need to improve on the most.

This is why I love my brother. He likes to gloat like the rest of us, but he's not satisfied unless he's getting better, even if it means taking one on the chin.

MIKE: My biggest concern is that the college student was bullying you around. As a novice, a bully is the guy you have to watch out for the most. A bully in poker is someone that bets so hard that the table thinks he's for real when he isn't, but everyone ends up folding after a few rounds of betting because he bets so strong. Since you weren't confident in your game, and you were uncomfortable about staying in against a guy betting so hard, you got bullied around by someone who had nothing in his hand. You were playing too many hands that you were wishy-washy about. That's how the bully took advantage of you. The dollar here and there that you threw into the pot before folding adds up over time.

JON: I didn't want to wait around like you were. Now I see what you mean about being patient. It isn't that easy. I'm not going to play that often, so I figured I might as well play a few more hands as long as I'm here.

MIKE: There's nothing wrong with doing what you did, but you most likely aren't going to win that way. Back to the bully for a second. The bully is my favorite player. He abuses everyone except me, because I don't play hands that are halfway. He can't bet me out of the game, which means he's just helping me make the pot bigger when I already have a good hand. Poker is all about attrition and waiting for that big hand. You have to minimize your losses while maximizing your gains. Think about it in baseball terms.

JON: Okay.

MIKE: Obviously, any home run is good, but a grand slam is a monster. In poker, if you hit a grand slam, you only have to win that hand the whole night to be a winner. You can hit a solo homer here and there, and maybe manufacture a few runs with singles and doubles, but it's best to smack one when guys are on base. That's how you're going to win. At the same time, you're going to lose more hands than win every time you play. A baseball player is going to get out more often then he gets on. You just don't want to go down swinging with men on base. You've gotta come up big when it matters and make

sure that when you do lose a hand the damage is as small as possible.
JON: I gotcha. You were totally in control at that table. You were by
far the best player. You absolutely killed those guys that were sitting
to my left. I was mightily impressed, bro. I'm not kidding. You've got
talent.
MIKE: Thanks, man. Those guys were hilarious. They were playing
every hand. I took about $40 from those guys alone. It was like tak-
ing candy from a baby. I love going up against those types of players.
JON: What would that be?
MIKE: The vacationer.
JON: Meaning?
MIKE: The vacationer is the everyday guy like you. He rarely gam-
bles and wants to enjoy his weekend in Vegas by playing, not watching. Professionals fold, vacationers play. Vacationers say to
themselves, "Well, I'm only going to be here for the weekend, so I
might as well play a few extra hands and hit the ATM one more time
if need be." Sort of like what you said. You can't play a few extra
hands in poker. Play a few more questionable hands and you'll be
seeing your stack of chips dwindle away. It might seem like they're
going down a little at a time, but you'll get up from the table $100
poorer because of it. As I said before, there's no halfway in poker.
You're in or you're out. You're winning or you're losing. If you're losing, you shouldn't be in the game. It's that simple. And vacationers
don't play that way. I don't blame them. I don't like coming to Vegas
and sitting on my ass either. But I know sitting on your ass and folding is the only way you're going to win consistently in poker.
JON: Let's get out of here. After we change our money, I think we
should head back to the hotel and wake those lazy asses up.
MIKE: Okay. I had fun playing with you.

We walked over to the cashier and handed the lady the chips that
we won at the poker table.

JON: Hey Mike, look at this poster for a poker tournament next
week at the Bellagio. It would be great if you could play in a tourna-

ment.

MIKE: It's during the week and it has a $750 entrance fee. I don't think it's for me. I've got my shitty job to look forward to, and it's an awful lot of money to just have a little fun. Although it would be nice to find out if I could hang with the big boys.

JON: Oh well. Let's get out of here. Thanks for showing me the ropes, Mike. I really enjoyed learning how to play.

CHAPTER 11

"Don't take life too serious. You'll never escape it alive anyway."

—Elbert Hubbard

Jon and I grabbed a quick snack before meeting Mark and Ben back at the hotel room at the Mirage. When we got back to the room, we talked about the poker game, and then began discussing what we should do for the night while watching a basketball game on television.

JON: Hey guys, have you seen my backpack. I need to grab something to read while I'm on the toilet.
BEN: What's in your backpack?
MIKE: There it is in the back corner. You're not gonna pull out a *Playboy* to take care of some "business" are you?
JON: Shut up, dude! I need to get my *Sports Illustrated*. Besides, I don't read *Playboy* anymore. I've moved on to better things, i.e. the Internet.
MIKE: Yeah, you and everyone else.... Actually, I'm a big fan of *Victoria Secret's*.
JON: I love that magazine.

BEN: Dude, it's a catalogue, not a magazine.

MARK: Uh, what are you, blind? You're obviously not getting as much pleasure out of it as we are. All I want them to do now is add a few articles, and I'll buy a subscription for the next five years.

MIKE: I don't need the articles. Their models are the most beautiful women in the world, for Christ's sake. I'd take the average *Victoria Secret's* girl over the hottest *Playboy* girl any day of the week. Of course, I still expect an invitation to the next party at The Mansion.

JON: I couldn't agree more…. There's my *Sports Illustrated*.

MARK: You gotta have an *SI* when you're on the can. I'd go so far as to say that I don't really enjoy going to the bathroom unless I have a *Sports Illustrated* with me. Whoa! I can't believe it hasn't come up yet. We got the cover, baby!

BEN: It's been on my mind since the start of the weekend, but I didn't want to bring it up. I'm so pissed that we're on the cover. Now there's no way we're going to win our bowl game.

MIKE: Why? The *SI* jinx? Yeah, you'd be an idiot to bet on Michigan now. *SI* has burned us too many times in the past to not take the Jinx seriously. I tried to keep it low profile as well. I figured Mark or Jon would bring it up the moment they stepped off the plane. Jon, you didn't think about *SI* at all until you had to take a crap. That's funny. When did you guys get your *SI* this week? Mine came on Thursday and I was a little pissed.

MARK: Why?

MIKE: Because Wednesday's early enough to still be thinking about and reevaluating the past week, but late enough to start getting pumped for the upcoming weekend. By the time Thursday rolls around, the previous game is in the past and all you're thinking about is the next one, so getting an *SI* after Wednesday is almost a waste.

MARK: True! I never really thought it through, but now that you mention it, I definitely notice a drop off in my interest if *SI* arrives after Wednesday during football season.

MIKE: Exactly.

MARK: It's the perfect day for a sports magazine. Everyone wants *SI* on Wednesday and everyone reads it on the toilet. You saw my bathroom last week when you came over. I had the four past issues of *SI* in my bathroom magazine rack.

MIKE: Yeah, I know. You and Jon are nuts about the magazine. Old school, dude.

JON: Old school? What the hell does that mean?

MIKE: It just means you guys are obsessed with the magazine. You guys should be in their commercials to promote the magazine.

BEN: They should film you guys on the toilet reading the magazine. I bet that's where most guys read it anyway, except for doctor's offices of course.

MIKE: That would be funny. The commercial starts off with something like, "As we all know, the biggest decisions we make are not in the boardroom, but in the bathroom." Then you go to someone like Mark or Jon, who is sitting on the toilet. They've got an *SI* in one hand and a *Wall Street Journal* in the other, and they're like, "Should I get up-to-date on sports or on my portfolio?" Of course, they choose *Sports Illustrated*.

JON: Do you think *SI* realizes that everyone reads the magazine while taking a dump?

MARK: I think they do. They probably sit in the boardroom with all the writers and the editors ask them what they got working for the next magazine issue. Then Rick Reilly says, "Well, I got my usual one-dumper on the back page, but I got a breaking story about this high school kid. It could easily be a three-dumper, maybe even a lead—I mean diarrhea worthy."

Speaking of Rick Reilly, he is probably the most popular writer for *Sports Illustrated*. He always has a one-page column on the last page of the magazine. Being one-page in length, his articles qualify as a quick read, i.e., a "one-dumper." One aspect of Reilly that makes him a great writer is that he says a lot in a small amount of space. Sometimes, Reilly's articles are humorous, while other times his articles are very serious, or even sad. Occasionally, he'll comment on a difficult issue, something like steroids in sports, or blow you over with an inspiring real-life story that is almost impossible to believe. Even though you often would think that his chosen subject matter is too vast or deep to adequately communicate in only a few paragraphs, he almost always manages to make his point. And there lies Reilly's excellence as a writer. He doesn't write just to tell you something; he writes to bring something to life. Not many writers try to make a real impact, and even fewer actually pull it off. Reilly does both. Check him out.

MIKE: Mark, this could be funny for a commercial. Then the editor goes, "Reilly, stick to your one-dumpers. That's your forte'. Our research has shown that people don't like being on the crapper for more than a one-dumper. That's why they enjoy your articles. They are short, but have a strong punch. Just like a quick dump. Pass your diarrhea story over to Zimmerman. He needs something to work on that will make him feel important, especially after those typical horrendous NFL predictions."

JON: That's hilarious, Mike. Do you guys always read Reilly first too?

MARK: Always Reilly. Usually, I'll come home, grab the mail, and then hit the toilet to read Reilly.

JON: No way. That's exactly what I did earlier this week. Every week, come to think of it. What do you read next?

MIKE: After Reilly, I finger through the first few pages to check out the full-page photos. I love those. After that, I try to hit "Go Figure."

BEN: I like the part when they say, "This Week's Sign of The Apocalypse." That always makes me laugh.

MARK: I'm exactly the same way. I try to hit the lead story after that, but sometimes I'm not interested in the lead story. One caveat. If it's like this week, and one of my teams or favorite players is the lead story, that will typically be the first thing I read after Reilly. Always Reilly first.

MIKE: I think that one of *SI's* flaws is that readers aren't interested in many of their articles. Of the five stories they have each week, I only want to read about three.

MARK: Not everyone has the same tastes. They have to cover all the sports, and sometimes there are great stories in the small sports...even hockey.

JON: You probably don't like to read the track or cross-country stories, but I dig that stuff. I know how dedicated and good those guys are since I used to run. I like reading those niche-oriented stories. *SI* fights for the little guys!

MIKE: I guess you're right. I don't read the whole sports page either.

BEN: Jon, are you going to the bathroom for a lead story or a Reilly? I think we should try to get out of here after you're done on the toilet.

JON: Most likely a Reilly, but you never know. I'm heading in.

MIKE: Okay, let's watch the end of this Jazz-Sonics game and then head somewhere for the night.

MARK: Sounds like a plan.

MIKE: Jon, wait. You gotta watch this! Did you see that pick and roll by Stockton and Malone? Classic!

JON: No one in the NBA does it better than them. That is in the NBA...

MIKE: True. No one does it better than the two of us. Not even Stockton and Malone. Our pick and roll is completely unstoppable in two-on-two.

MARK: Will you guys stop talking about your freaking crappy two-on-two streak? Every time I see you guys, you bring it up. It's getting old.

MIKE: I would be annoyed too if I had lost 30 games in a row to the same team. What's our streak at now, Jon?

JON: Not exactly sure. It's definitely over 60 games in a row. We haven't lost since you were in high school. That's at least nine years ago.

MIKE: Damn, a 9-year winning streak…. I thought going unde-feated one year was impressive, but nine years, that is definitely say-ing something special.

MARK: Dude, you guys have beaten players like Ben for half of your wins. If you played any competition, you wouldn't have won a game in 10 years.

JON: You were Ben's teammate for about half those wins. And you claim to be the best in the family.

MARK: I don't claim to be the best. I am the best.

MIKE: Yet, we beat you every time. That should show you that there really is something special about our streak. That there is more to it than just talent that propels us to victory. We keep winning, even when we are so-called overmatched against you and whoever your teammate is.

MARK: Whatever. I don't want to hear the story again. You've said it a million times.

JON: I'd be up for a million and one. But first things first. Now, will you guys let me take my Reilly in peace, please?

CHAPTER 12

"It's not the size of the dog in the fight, it's the size of the fight in the dog."

—Mark Twain

I wouldn't have subjected my brothers to yet another rendition of the streak, but I will relate the legend to you. The story of my two-on-two basketball streak with Jon began in the summer of 1991 when I was in 10th grade. I was in high school and Jon was home from college for the summer. All our friends made regular appearances on the court on our driveway, but our most frequent opponents were Fred and Chris. My friend Fred was 6'1" and 200 pounds. He was the biggest of the bunch already and good enough to play high school basketball. Chris is Jon's friend, and is best described as your typical suburban white kid ballplayer. A few good moves, a little slow, but hustles, and overall plays a smart game.

The summer was typical in that, like every summer of my childhood, basketball ruled. It was late June when Jon and I first realized we hadn't lost in a while. We figured that we had probably won about ten games in a row and started to get a little cocky. We weren't getting in our friends faces or anything. That isn't cool. We were pestering them just enough to get into their heads. It's important to know exactly how far you can go with your friends and to be very careful not to cross that thin line. Then, one hot, sunny afternoon, the little streak that we had taken note of officially became THE STREAK.

Fred and Chris were dying to put an end to our run. They wanted blood. They were looking forward to the next game far more than Jon and I could have anticipated. When we checked the ball, we all knew that this game was going to set the tone for the rest of the summer. There was plenty of pride on the line, and pride goes far when you're playing with friends. Jon would cover Fred, and I would cover Chris. They had size. We had speed.

Game was to 11. Pass-in rule. Air balls always have to be taken back. Winners-out. Win by two.

As soon as the game started, it felt like Game 7 of the NBA Championship. The score was tied at three, four, five, and then six. No one would budge. The game was that tight. Then Fred and Chris went on a surge, scoring four quick baskets to put our streak in jeopardy. It was point-game. If they made one more shot, they would win and end our streak. Jon and I were completely shocked. They began to taunt us, thrilled to be the architects of the end of our streak. Unlike Jon and I, they were totally in our faces. Not cool. But right after their tenth basket dropped, the initial shock to Jon and I quickly transformed into confidence. We knew we were better, and we knew this game was just getting started. This was the moment that everything changed. Something clicked. We suddenly acquired an aura of invincibility—a necessary ingredient of a streak—that most people don't experience in an entire lifetime. We refused to lose. The beauty was that our opponents had the ball and we still felt that way.

Before Jon checked the ball, we looked into each other's eyes. Focus and determination beamed forth. No words needed to be spoken; our expressions said it all. Jon checked up, and Chris took a running jumper that hit the rim and went out of bounds. We made the stop. Now we had the ball.

Jon checked up, and dished the ball over to me on the left 15 feet from the hoop. I didn't even hesitate...swish...10-7. *No fear.*

Jon checked up again. He passed me the ball at the same spot. This time I pump faked, my favorite move, and blew by Chris for my patented underhand lay-up. 10-8. *No worries.*

It was gut check time for Fred and Chris. They needed a defensive stand. They never got it.

Jon blew by Fred, was fouled by Chris, and still made his drive to the basket. 10-9. *No Problem.*

Jon then scored again on a sweet back door cut for an easy lay-up. 10-10. *Next.*

We went 4-4, made a defensive stand, and all this happened in less than 10 minutes. The game was over and our opponents knew it. They didn't have the will that Jon and I had cultivated as a team. I sunk the 11th basket and Jon finished it off with an easy drive to the hole. 12-10. We won. They never even touched the ball again. THE STREAK was born.

The beauty of our streak is that Jon and I to this day still have that aura of invincibility when we play; the sense that there's no way we are going to lose. Losing isn't an option. And this is in the face of competition that would like nothing more than to put our streak to an end. Of course, people always want to win, but when there's a streak involved there's that extra bit of incentive. It's like when an NBA player has an opportunity to play against Michael Jordan. They bring their "A" game knowing that he's the best in the world. They would love to be the ones to knock him off his pedestal. Jordan, on the other hand, like many streakholders, views his competition as simply another roadblock in his way. Streakholders don't care who they face. Their competition should just stand in line and take a number.

My streak with my brother means a lot more to me than just a simple statistic. The Streak is special because it reminds me that the bond of brotherhood can overcome the presence of more talent. Our wins have plenty to do with skill, but the length and consistency of the Streak is mostly about heart, dedication, trust, and faith. All the intangibles that can't be measured, yet always seem to be present in true champions at any level. If I wasn't playing with my brother, the Streak would have ended that day or some time soon thereafter. The Streak still lives though, and now even garners the respect of Fred and Chris, who in part are responsible for making the Streak what it is today.

SUNDAY

CHAPTER 13

"Keep away from people who belittle your ambitions. Small people always do that, but the really great, make you feel that you too can become great."

—Mark Twain

We spent the rest of Saturday night gambling our money away and reminiscing about when we were younger. I checked my voicemail the next morning, expecting to get a message from the mechanic who was working on my car.

Instead, I received a call from my boss, informing me that the company had decided to lay-off numerous employees and I was one of them. He said I needn't even bother coming into work and that I would receive two-weeks severance. The guy laid me off by voicemail! What a wuss. I started to get into a bit of a panic. Two weeks was not going to get me very far. How can anyone expect to find a new job in two weeks?

The truth is that being laid-off was the first step in my ultimate decision to take some time off from Corporate America in order to figure out what I really wanted to do with my life. I suddenly had the time to get away like Jon and I had talked about the day before. The only thing I still needed was a huge sum of cash.

Jon woke up and I played the voice message for him. He was sympathetic, but at the same time, we both knew that the writing was on the wall. We went downstairs to grab a cup of coffee and to discuss my new predicament.

"I think I'm going to go for it."

"Go for what? What are you talking about?"

"I'm going to enter the poker tournament at the Bellagio on Wednesday."

"Dude, you need to relax for a moment. You've probably got all kinds of adrenaline flowing, and now you're going into overdrive because you just got two weeks vacation. Don't go making any extreme decisions. Let's talk this through for a minute."

"I've thought it through. The tournament is on Wednesday. I'll just chill here for a couple of days, play a bit of poker to hone my skills, and then I'll play in the tournament and leave as soon as it's over."

"Where are you going to stay? You can't afford to stay at the hotels out here by yourself."

"I'll just stay off the Strip. That shouldn't be a problem."

"Mike, two weeks is not a long time to find a job. You'll be burning cash a lot quicker then you think. You'll be broke in a month or two."

"True, but the four days here won't make a difference in the long-run. Plus, I can win the tournament."

"I saw you play and you were good. But a tournament? You'll be going against professionals, not chumps like me. Not to mention the fact that the entrance fee is $750. That's $750 you can use to live on while you're looking for a job. You'll need that money."

"I know. $750 is a lot of money. I said I think I'm going to go for it, but I'm not sure just yet. I can definitely still be swayed against it."

"Do you know how tournaments work?"

"Tournaments are a little different than the normal type of game that we played yesterday. It's pretty difficult to explain, but I know all the rules. My biggest disadvantage will be that I lack tournament experience. I would expect that, if anything, to be my downfall."

"I don't know, bro. You got a good thing going right now with your occasional trips to Vegas. Playing in the tournament might be a little too much."

"Yeah, I know it's big stakes. But you know what, our whole lives we're always watching professional sports on television. We always dream of being in the game, and making the big shot. Now, I have that chance. I can't do it in football or basketball, but in poker I have the chance to not only play but to win. I think I can compete with the big boys. I really want to find out. I think $750 is a lot, but it's worth it to find out if I'm as good as I believe I am."

"I hear what you're saying. On the upside, I guess, if you somehow manage to win you'll have money to travel…and then some."

"That's one of the main reasons why I want to play. I want to win that cash so I can take that trip we talked about. Whenever I think about it, I feel myself get excited. I haven't felt that way about anything in a long time, and I know that if I don't act on it the excitement will pass."

"I think that's really true. You've got to act when you have the inclination. Otherwise, it'll pass. Life will take over, and before you know it, you're back at square one. A 9 to 5 job that you don't like, wishing you had the guts to take a risk."

"Right. If I'm not willing to take a risk in my early twenties, I definitely won't be taking one when I'm forty. That's not how I want to live my life."

"I guess I can't stop someone who wants a chance at playing in the big game. I'd be proud of you for stepping up. Not everyone wants to find out how good they really are because most of the time you know deep down that you aren't good enough. I have to tell you something. Sometimes I ask people, just to get some insight into what type of person they are, whether they'd want to be on the foul line at the end of the game or whether they'd prefer a teammate to take the last shot. Most people don't want it, even if they think they do. I've always said that something I admire about you is that not only do you want the last shot, but I'd be confident you would make it. Win or lose, I've got your back."

"Thanks."

"Let's make a deal."

"What's that?"

"If you win, go on a trip like we've talked about. If you lose, take a break from poker until you're financially secure in your next job. What do you think about that?"

"Doesn't sound like a bad idea. I'll mull it over."

"Listen, to show you that I totally believe in you, I'm going to give you $250 to help you out. I saw a few flashes of brilliance when we played. I actually think you've got a shot. If you win, just give me $250 from your winnings, and if you lose you pay me back when you can. You play your way."

"Thanks bro. That means a lot to me. I can't believe I'm going to enter one of these tournaments. Three years ago, I would never have thought that I would be in this situation. For that matter, I wouldn't have guessed anything right about my life. Life is somewhat crazy."

"Sure is bro, sure is. The twenties are an extra crazy time in your life. I can tell you from my own experience. But enjoy the tournament, win or lose. Go out and have fun."

"I guess I won't be making my flight later today!"

"Yeah, guess not! Let's go up to the room and have lunch before everyone has to go. I wish I could be there to watch you play. You know I'll be there in spirit."

THE TOURNAMENT

CHAPTER 14

"The smarter you play, the luckier you'll be."

—Mark Pilarski

I won't go into every detail about the tournament and my performance. It was emotionally draining. I'll leave it at that. The games were much more intense than I even imagined. The competition was tough. I was nervous early on, so I played conservative. As my confidence grew, I opened up my game. I went after a couple of flushes and straights and fortunately picked them up when I needed to. I knew going for those types of hands would be risky because they put me in an all-or-nothing proposition. I would either win big or lose hard. I was overmatched, so I had to take a few more chances than usual to survive. It was to no avail. I didn't win the tournament. I didn't even finish in the top ten. However, I did finish in the top 30, which gave me $9,000 in prize money!

Next to the prize money, the most rewarding part of the tourney was that I did find answers about my poker game. I was a great player, but I was far from being the best. Poker is too hard of a game to conquer that quickly. It's similar to golf, where most people make great strides early to improve their game, but after a certain point, improving their score by a stroke or two is very difficult to do. I still went way beyond my expectations.

Now, with the spoils of my success, I had a six-month trip to Asia to plan! I would have the chance to sort out my future, enjoy a long break, and hopefully get closer to finding the answers to the true questions we all must face. I wasn't sure if I was going to find them out there in Asia. Hell, I didn't even know what I would be doing out there, but I knew that traveling can free your mind.

My crazy week was finally about to come to a close. Before it ended, I called Jon. I told him what happened in the tournament, and I thanked him for helping me seize an opportunity that I normally wouldn't have taken. There was no guarantee that I was going to win in the tournament—I could have lost my shirt—but very few things in life are certain. You have to give life your utmost effort, and only then can you look back and say that you did your very best.

THE TRIP

CHAPTER 15

"Life isn't about finding yourself. Life is about creating your-self."

—George Bernard Shaw

Immediately after college, I had the luxury of backpacking in Europe with Mark and Ben. During my trip, I kept a diary, and thoroughly enjoyed the process of writing down my thoughts. One of the things you learn when you travel for a long period is how you manage your down time. Writing in my diary and playing countless hours of Gin Rummy with my brothers filled mine. Down time is not an easy concept for some people to handle. Many people, especially Americans, have the need to always be busy, and become so bored by all the down time that is endemic to long periods of travel that they decide to return home. It may therefore surprise many people that I found the down time with my brothers to be the most rewarding aspect of our trip.

At the outset of my trip to Asia, I filled my down time by reading numerous books and writing in my diary. After about a month of traveling, however, I found that I wasn't getting anything out of the diary. It wasn't bringing me any satisfaction. I was spending so much time writing about what I did on my travels that I rarely addressed the more important questions about what I thought or how I really felt. The diary wasn't taking me to the deeper level which I wanted and needed to reach on this trip. So, I decided to stop writing, and read more instead.

I tried to read in exotic locations that provided me with an opportunity to clear my mind and think naturally and freely about my life ahead, all the while enjoying a good book. My favorite spots were at the ruins of Angkor Wat in Cambodia, the caves at Vang Vien in Laos, and on the incredible and fascinating islands of Thailand. What I started to realize from reading these books was that the authors were writing things that described precisely how I felt. Many of the novels I read were modern fiction—stories that could be real, but obviously involved fictional characters. I felt I had something in common with all of these characters, and because of that, the books lent me peace of mind. The authors managed to make me feel more comfortable about how my life had transpired. They made me realize that I wasn't the only one who felt this way about life.

Inspired by all my reading, I felt that instead of simply writing about my travels, I could write something about myself by telling a story that seemed relevant to my generation. It felt great to put something down on paper. I had written once before for my college newspaper when I was a freshman, and seeing my name in the byline was extremely rewarding. I honestly didn't really care what other people thought about my work. I had accomplished a task that the editors thought was worthy of print.

After writing a few pieces during my travels, I decided to send one of the stories to Jon via email. Jon really enjoyed the story (partly because he thought the story made him the main character) and told me that he saw some promise. He suggested that I keep on writing and see where it would take me. I wasn't writing every day, but by the end of my trip I had already written most of the stories that form the backbone of this book.

The trip itself was the most incredible experience of my life. After spending a few months in planning, I traveled through Asia for over six months. I started in China and then headed over to South East Asia, where I spent the majority of my time. I was able to see the Great Wall, the Forbidden City, and the magnificent temples of Angkor Wat. I trekked and rode elephants in Northern Thailand, rode tubes down rivers in Laos, explored incredible ancient caves, rock-climbed cliffs, and relaxed on the sublime islands of Thailand. Most importantly, I got a small taste of life on the other side of the globe. I sometimes wish it could have been longer, although I usually think I went away for the perfect amount of time. Traveling for six months gave me enough time to feel like I truly got away, without straying so far (both in time and space) from my "regular" life that I would be entirely disoriented upon my return home.

One of the most important things traveling can do for an individual is to provide a different perspective on life. I quickly realized, not in an abstract way but first-hand, that luxury items, like hot showers, air-conditioning, and expensive clothing, are things that make our lives more comfortable and enjoyable, but in the end, really aren't that important. This point was driven home on a number of occasions. I caught a lift one afternoon from a cabby whose "taxi" was nothing more than a bicycle with a chair attached to the front. Walking back from the bar that night, I found him asleep on that same bicycle, which evidently doubled as his home. Very often, I would see little girls and amputees begging for money, or meet locals who have never been more than three miles outside their hometown. If I didn't already know it, these experiences made it very clear how spoiled I was back home. It forced me to recognize that even if I was at the worst point of my life, I would still have it much easier than many people in this world.

CHAPTER 16

"A pessimist sees the difficulty in every opportunity; an optimist sees the opportunity in every difficulty."

—Sir Winston Churchill

While I had numerous experiences during my trip that I will always cherish, there were two specific, and totally opposite events that had the most dramatic effect on my career and my outlook on life. After traveling through China and much of Thailand, I decided I needed to rest for a while, and headed to the islands in Southern Thailand to relax on the beaches. Having spent two weeks on Koh Samui and Koh Phangan, I headed to the island of Koh Tao, known to be the most laid-back of the three. While Koh Phangan is popular for its partying and especially the infamous Full Moon Party, Koh Tao is a haven for scuba divers and those seeking diver certification.

I disembarked from the boat with the other backpackers, and, as usual, the locals were more than anxious to greet us. After giving my best effort to evade the routine harassment by the parade of locals, whose only aim is to convince you that you should stay at their bungalow, I made my home at the Sunshine Bungalow on the Southern end of the island. Each bungalow is similar to a tiny resort that accommodates all your needs. You sleep in their cozy huts, eat at their lovely ocean-side restaurant, and take scuba classes with their exceptional instructors. You don't have to do all these activities at your bungalow, but it only makes sense since it's cheaper and easier. The only significant reason to leave your mini-resort, other than to take a stroll or visit a friend, is to sample the dining fare at the other bungalow's restaurants (something I did quite often).

It had been a hectic day getting to the island, and my four-day scuba class didn't start until the following afternoon. I decided to get a good night sleep. When I awoke in the morning, I was definitely fresh. It was a beautiful day outside; I could take in a bit of sun in the morning and would make my way to scuba class in the afternoon. Before I suntanned, I wanted to have breakfast, so I made the 15-yard walk from my hut to the bungalow restaurant. There is nothing better than making your world small, which is exactly what happens on these islands. I think this is one reason why people love to go to resorts. Making the world small simplifies your existence, and some-how, everything that you normally think about is forgotten until you eventually leave your brief utopia.

I grabbed a seat at one of the tables. There were a few other people eating as well. I read a book until the waiter came over and took my order. I asked for banana pancakes. When you order banana pan-cakes at home, what do you expect? Pancakes with bananas crushed inside or chopped on top. Not here. The "chef" basically just plopped an entire banana atop my stack of flapjacks. It was as if I said, "Can I have pancakes AND a banana." Why do they call it banana pancakes if they aren't going to mush them together? Why don't they list them as separate items on the menu? Am I right or just a little anal?

As I was eating my food, a stunningly beautiful girl walked into the restaurant and sat at the table next to mine. She was facing my direction. I would guess that the tables were approximately 5-10 feet apart. This girl was perfect. She was roughly 5'6", with beautiful long dark hair. She appeared to be in great shape, and was wearing a bikini with a t-shirt. The girl was the best of both worlds. She was cute and sexy at the same time. Not many girls are able to pull it off, but she was more than up to the task. She was wearing sunglasses, and I couldn't tell if she was one of those girls who wear sunglasses because they're less attractive without them. Luckily for me, when she took them off her eyes only made her more beautiful. I started to get a little nervous, knowing that my ideal girl was right in front of my face. What could possibly be better than being with your dream girl on a beautiful secluded island? Was I going to step to the plate and talk to her or was I going to wimp out?

She ordered her meal, an omelet with toast and jelly, and I noticed that she sounded American. Her accent was exactly like a friend I knew from New Jersey. I know you're probably thinking, "Yikes, strike one," but she was one of those Jersey girls who didn't grow up right off the Turnpike and therefore managed to avoid the "Your from Jersey? Me too, which exit?" stereotype. Now, being American might not seem like a big deal when you're in the States, but when you're traveling abroad you quickly learn that, in general, Americans do not travel to certain destinations nearly as much as people from other countries do. In a strange way, I felt that when I did meet an American, I was compelled to talk to them. I guess I yearned on some level for a connection with my American identity and for that foundation which I would only have with someone, anyone, from the United States. I should be careful not to over-state this point, though, since one of the craziest things that I realized while abroad is that the world is a great deal smaller than we might believe, even when you're as far away as South East Asia. For example, while on a boat in Cambodia from Phnom Penh, the capital, to Siem Reap, I ran into an old baseball buddy who I used to play with 10 years ago. He lived 15 minutes from my parent's house and we never once ran into each other in our hometown. Now, in the middle of Cambodia, we recognized each other and spent a few days together before going our separate ways. How wild is that?

Back to the girl. I was about to finish my meal, but I knew I didn't want to leave the restaurant before at least employing some tactic that would allow me to attempt to talk to this girl. She appeared to be alone, meaning two things. One, she probably did not have a boyfriend, and two, men would soon be all over her. The best part about her at this particular moment was that, despite her beauty, she seemed to be approachable. How can I tell whether a girl is approachable? To be honest, there really isn't a formula. I just have a gut feeling. All guys do. For example, Britney Spears would be approachable while Christina Aguilera wouldn't. Sarah Jessica Parker would chat with you, while Tara Reid wouldn't give you the time of day. Jennifer Love Hewitt would listen to what you have to say, while Jennifer Lopez would shake her ass and walk away. Sandra Bullock would act like she enjoyed your company, while Elizabeth Hurley would laugh at your fruitless attempts. There's no logical basis for my assessment, but I think you would agree with it.

My brain was trying to think of anything to say, but my dick was telling me to say anything. As I said before, she wasn't right next to me, and I didn't want to come across like an idiot by shouting across the restaurant. After all, there were other people around. I couldn't just go up and grab a seat either. Well I could, but I didn't think it was appropriate to disturb a totally random person while they were eating a meal in peace.

I started to look for angles that I could use to spark a conversation. I noticed that she had a book on her table, so I naturally considered the standard, but very reliable "Hey, what book are you reading?" approach. The book pickup line is an easy one to use while traveling because people are often reading popular titles. Unfortunately, I couldn't see the title, so that route was foreclosed. I was stymied.

Incidentally, the book pickup line can be a great conversation starter in other settings, especially for college students. I originally learned the line from my brother Mark, who in his college days would bring a cool book he was reading (or had already read) when he went to the library to study. Mark would find a seat at a table where a cute girl was studying, preferably alone. He would then place his book, or should I say bait, in a position such that the title of the book would be in plain view, all the while making sure that the book blended in with his textbooks. Let me give you an example of a typical scene:

Mark notices an attractive woman studying by herself at a table, and walks over to the table to sit down. Before grabbing a seat, he asks the girl for permission. This is a must. It initiates contact, all the while demonstrating class and manners.

"Hey, do you mind if I sit here? The library is pretty crowded today."
"Yeah, sure. Not a problem at all. Sorry for the mess."
"Oh, don't worry about it. Thanks for making room."

Mark takes his textbooks out of his bag and leaves *High Fidelity*, a highly popular contemporary book and film, in a position where it will definitely be noticed. After studying for a half-hour, Mark grabs the copy of *High Fidelity* and starts flipping through the pages to see where he left off the last time he picked it up.

"Hey, have you ever seen the movie?"
"*High Fidelity*?"
"Yeah."
"It's one of my favorite movies. I'm a big fan of John Cusack. I've never read the book though. Is it good?"
"The book is great. I can't put it down. Unfortunately, I have to study for this stupid Organic Chemistry test that's coming up in a few days."
"Pre-Med?"

"Yeah. I want to be a doctor, but after Organic Chemistry I'm not so sure."

"Oh, don't worry about it. My brother is a doctor and he said that Organic Chemistry is a complete waste of time."

"That's cool. What type of doctor is your brother?"

You catch my drift. Mark completely captured her attention by using the book as a conversation starter. He was a smooth operator. He first emphasized his studies, and then took a strategic break to chat. If the girl wasn't interested, he'd just take off for a bit and check his email at the computer center. No harm done.

Now, if the girl was a lot more difficult, then Mark would have had to take a somewhat different approach, but overall would employ the same strategy.

"Hey, have you ever the movie?"

"*High Fidelity*?

"Yeah."

"No. Why?"

Asking *why* is a sure sign that she isn't looking to get hit on at the library. But don't worry. The game is still afoot. My brother has skills.

"Oh, I'm just about to finish the book and I wanted to see if the movie was worth renting."

"Sorry. Wish I could help you but I haven't seen it yet."

"Don't worry about it."

Mark reads the final 20 pages of the book, giving himself more credibility.

"Don't you feel sad when you finish a great book?"

"You're done? How was it?"

"It was incredible. You should really read it when you get a chance."

"Oh, I wish I had the time. I love to read, but during the school year I seem to only have time to read my textbooks."

"I hear ya…. What class are you studying for now?"

"Social Psychology."

"With Morris?"

"Yeah. Did you take that class already?"

"Yeah. I'm getting a minor in Psychology. I loved that class."

It took another conversation, but Mark got what he wanted out of the book. It's true; patience is a virtue.

Anyway, returning to the woman at the restaurant. After a few more minutes, I determined that the book angle was dead. It just didn't seem right. I was starting to get a little tense because I knew I had a clear shot at this girl. I just needed to figure out the best approach.

Then, out of the blue, a dog trotted over to her table. In Thailand, stray dogs run rampant. They lie around the hostels, beaches, and bungalows looking for scraps of food. While they seem to be friendly creatures, they are disgustingly dirty dogs that aren't taken care of at all. This particular stray went to her table and, within a few seconds, I could tell that she had affection for dogs. I love dogs, and I like women who like dogs. Plus, and more on point, I have several dog stories in my repertoire that can be utilized, when needed, to initiate conversations with women. In other words, I had an "in." I don't want to suggest that I was hoping to use the dog, or that I saw the animal as nothing more than a tool, but everyone knows that dogs can be the perfect wingman. Case in point, guys taking their dogs to the park on a beautiful summer day!

All of a sudden, there was a loud noise and the dog ran off. I immediately realized that my golden opportunity just turned to lead. How can the dog just leave me like that! You can't leave your wingman! Hasn't the dog seen *Top Gun*! Everyone has seen *Top Gun*! The dog left me out to croak. I couldn't believe it. Now, my second angle had been sabotaged. Of course, this is all going on in my head; she had no clue what I was thinking. She was probably thinking she should have ordered the banana pancakes, while I was trying to figure out what I would do with her if I got her in bed!

Then my wingman came back! He didn't leave me after all. He heard the noise and veered off for a minute, but sensing that I needed help, returned to the battle like a true wingman should. This time, when the dog approached her table, she tried to give the dog some food. Now that my wingman was exchanging friendly fire, I sat back and analyzed his maneuvers in order to assess my next line of attack. The girl grabbed a piece of toast with a spread of jelly on top. Stray dogs in Thailand will eat almost any food they can get their mouths on. However, for some reason my wingman wasn't grabbing the food she was offering. He was sniffing it, but something was holding him back.

My wingman had done it! He had given me the signal to move in without uttering a single word! I always said that non-verbal communication speaks louder than words! Employing my arsenal of experiences with dogs, I knew that many dogs don't like fruit. I figured the dog wasn't eating the bread because of the jelly.

I knew this was my chance, probably my only chance. My wingman gave me an opening, now I just had to hit the target. But what I was about to say was risky. If I said, "The dog doesn't like the jelly," and then he refused to eat a plain piece of bread, I would look like a fool. I was putting myself on the line. On the flip side, if I was right, this girl should be pretty freaking impressed (to the degree that anyone could be at this point), because I took a chance and demonstrated right from the get go that I'm for real. I wasn't just dropping a pickup line to talk to her. I was actually helping her feed a sad, impoverished puppy.

I decided to go with, "The dog doesn't like the jelly on the bread. Try a plain piece." Fire! She acknowledged my response with, "Oh really." She grabbed a new, plain piece of bread and handed it toward the dog. As in any major military engagement, everything shifted into slow motion as I waited for my missile to hit. The dog started sniffing, and with a slight jerk of his head, he snatched the food! He shoots, he scores! She looked at me, squinting slightly in contemplation, and said, "You were right. How did you know that?" I mentioned that my old dog would never eat fruit because it's too sweet. After chatting for a minute or two, I asked her if I could move to her table. She consented and we continued our conversation!

Incredibly, she was not just American, but actually lived in the Bay Area. More importantly yet, she was also a teacher. She was originally from the East Coast, as I had guessed, and moved out West when she went to college at Berkeley. We spent the week together on the island, and while no romance ensued, a great friendship was born. I talked to her about my teaching aspirations, and she couldn't stop talking about how much she loved to teach. She even mentioned that she could probably get me an interview at the high school she worked at since they were in desperate need for teachers. Since we both still had a lot of time left on our trips, we exchanged emails and agreed that when we both got back, we would meet up and set a time for me to interview with the principal at her school.

CHAPTER 17

"When the people we love are stolen from us the thing we have to remember is to never stop loving them. Buildings burn. People die, but true love is forever."

—The Crow

While my new female friend eventually had a huge effect on my career path, an event back home enlightened me to what was truly important in life. A couple of months after enjoying the beaches in Thailand, I found my way over to Saigon, Vietnam. One early evening, upon returning from a two-day Mekong Delta tour, I decided to check my email at an Internet café near my hostel. During my travels, I used AOL Instant Messenger as an efficient and economical method of communication in order to stay in touch with my family and friends. I was talking to one of my buddies on IM when the first plane hit the World Trade Center. When he told me the news about the first plane, I knew it was tragic, but I thought it was just an accident, so I went back to the hostel and didn't think much of it. A couple of hours later, after speaking with a few more people, I learned a second plane had hit the other tower. I quickly recognized that this wasn't an accident at all, and headed back to the Internet café to hopefully find my brother Jon online. We had the most frequent communication while on my trip because he always had IM loaded at his desk at work.

The following transcript is the IM conversation Jon and I had a few hours after the first plane hit the World Trade Center. Jon kept a copy of our exchange, knowing how meaningful and unique the transcript of our conversation would be. Jon worked in downtown Boston.

Jontlwy: Mike.
Mikezly: Jon.
Mikezly: I'm so glad you're online.
Jontlwy: This is unbelievable.
Mikezly: Dude, what the hell? Have u talked to everyone? Dad and mom?
Jontlwy: I haven't talked to anyone.
Jontlwy: It is impossible to get through.
Mikezly: Are u still at work?
Jontlwy: I've been trying to reach Dad, but can't get through.
Jontlwy: I'm at work.
Mikezly: Is that near any big buildings and such?
Jontlwy: All tall buildings in Boston shut down.
Jontlwy: No big buildings nearby.
Mikezly: Good.
Jontlwy: This is very scary.
Jontlwy: The T is closed. People are meandering about. They can't get home.
Mikezly: I have a friend that works near the world trade center. His dad works in it frequently.
Jontlwy: Holy crap. Any word?
Jontlwy: Are you on with anyone else right now?
Jontlwy: I'm getting through to home, but no one is picking up.
Mikezly: I'm online only with you. They wouldn't let my friend out, so he was telling me, then I asked about his bro and dad, and he started talking and then was just gone. He signed off…

Jontlwy: I realized I can only get through with my calling card.

Mikezly: I don't know where he went.

Jontlwy: That is scary with your friend. Let me know if you hear from him.

Mikezly: What has been bombed? Recap anything new.

Jontlwy: Just left a message at home.

Mikezly: With dad and mom?

Jontlwy: Yes.

Jontlwy: Here's the recap. Some of this is not certain, only what I've heard. It's all sketchy.

Jontlwy: World trade building, both towers are gone.

Jontlwy: All people on first plane are dead.

Jontlwy: Camp David, bombed.

Jontlwy: State Dept. car bomb.

Jontlwy: Pentagon, bombed by airplane.

Jontlwy: Four airplanes missing.

Jontlwy: People were jumping out of the world trade center.

Jontlwy: They just crumbled into dust.

Mikezly: Oh my god.

Jontlwy: Airplane crashed near Pittsburgh.

Jontlwy: Ash 3 inches thick across Manhattan.

Jontlwy: Debris is flying across Brooklyn, papers, glass, etc.

Jontlwy: Are people there aware of what's happening yet?

Mikezly: Only some Americans have taken an interest. No one really knows.

Mikezly: I shouldn't leave Vietnam?

Jontlwy: You're better off in SE Asia.

Jontlwy: Historic monuments are being preserved.

Mikezly: Should I go to Cambodia?

Jontlwy: I would stay put for a day or so.

Jontlwy: DC is in major panic.

Jontlwy: I'm glad you're on.

Jontlwy: Wish other people had IM.

Mikezly: This is crazy.

Jontlwy: Until recently, people were still hanging by the White House for a tour.

Jontlwy: They didn't know anything had happened.

Mikezly: This is the scariest thing I have ever heard.

Jontlwy: This is the worst attack ever in the US.

Jontlwy: This could be WWIII.

A few minutes later.

Mikezly: Dad would be working in Virginia today, right?

Mikezly: It would seem likely that they would go for another spot.

Jontlwy: Definitely.

Jontlwy: The one near Pittsburgh was strange.

Jontlwy: I'm wondering if the captain just crashed the plane when they tried to hijack it.

Jontlwy: That plane was going to LA.

Mikezly: Call 703-555-1234 for Dad's office.

Jontlwy: 92 people on the second world trade center plane all dead.

Jontlwy: I can't get through.

Mikezly: Where did the plane land in NYC?

Mikezly: If it hit the towers it had to land somewhere.

Jontlwy: None landed. Crashed right into the top of the world trade center and then went down.

Jontlwy: The planes basically exploded on impact.

Jontlwy: Mike, so many people are dead.

Jontlwy: Could be 1000s.

Jontlwy: 50,000 people work in the world trade center.

Jontlwy: This is worse than Pearl Harbor.

Mikezly: I'm so scared for everyone.

Mikezly: I'm crying.

Jontlwy: Me too.

Mikezly: Holy crap.

Jontlwy: I'm sort of holding it together b/c I'm at work.

Jontlwy: People are pretty freaked.

Mikezly: Try calling everyone in the family. I want to know if everyone is fine.

Jontlwy: I already have. Just can't through and no one is picking up
when I do.

Jontlwy: Wait a minute. I'll be back.

A few minutes later.

Jontlwy: Mike.

Mikezly: J I'm here.

Jontlwy: Hey.

Mikezly: My friend who works near the world trade center and his
dad are fine.

Mikezly: I just spoke via IM. He is back online in his apartment.

Jontlwy: That's good news.

Mikezly: Have u spoke to dad and mom?

Jontlwy: I'm getting through to people, just not them.

Mikezly: Have u tried 301-555-8764?

Jontlwy: Yeah.

Mikezly: I just thought of another friend that works downtown. I'm
scared again.

Jontlwy: I'm just scared since we don't even know where/how to
defend ourselves.

Mikezly: Can u do me a favor, when you have a chance call 555-4321,
or tell mom and dad to do it. That's Robin Dexter's #. Tell her to
email me if she is all right.

Jontlwy: Are you ok? I'll do it.

Mikezly: You know my email.

Mikezly: I'm ok.

Mikezly: But I'm just sad for everyone.

Mikezly: And hope people I know are okay.

Mikezly: They killed possibly 50,000.

Jontlwy: I know.

Jontlwy: The news coverage brought me to tears. It was frightening to see the buildings crumble.

Mikezly: That's more than Pearl Harbor. Vietnam was 70,000.

Jontlwy: I know.

Mikezly: Did the whole building just fall to the ground? How much is damaged, like floors 20 and up or what?

Jontlwy: The whole thing is gone.

Jontlwy: Both towers.

Mikezly: Gone, like not there at all?

Mikezly: Or just half a building?

Jontlwy: It started crumbling at the top and all went down. All gone. Not just half. All gone.

Jontlwy: People were jumping out of windows to get away from the fire.

Mikezly: From how high up? What?

Jontlwy: A plane went clean thru, and left a whole. Then 2 hours later it toppled. Makes no sense.

Jontlwy: I'm on the phone with Mark. Mark says hang in there.

Jontlwy: You will be fine.

Jontlwy: Mark doesn't want you to travel anywhere, neither do I.

Mikezly: All right.

Mikezly: Yeah, I'll stay put for now.

Jontlwy: Mark will try to get on tonight to talk to you.

Jontlwy: Mike, I'll be back in 5 minutes. A co-worker needs me.

Mikezly: OK. Comeback.

Jontlwy: Will do.

Five minutes later.

Jontlwy: Mike. They are saying they think it was led by Osama Bin Laden.

Mikezly: Who's that?

Jontlwy: Osama Bin Laden was the guy who masterminded the bombing of the world trade center last time.

Mikezly: And he was never found?

Jontlwy: We never found him, but we know where he is and that he was behind it.

Mikezly: No traces or anything? Where is he from? What group?

Jontlwy: He's considered Public Enemy #1 in the U.S.

Mikezly: Country?

Jontlwy: We know that he has been hiding in different places, including Afghanistan.

Jontlwy: He was likely in Libya for a while, but fled.

Mikezly: Any political ties?

Jontlwy: He's wily as crap. And extremely rich.

Jontlwy: Some hard line Muslim movement. I forget which one.

Mikezly: What do u think is going to happen in the next few days?

Jontlwy: We'll try to figure out what happened, see who takes responsibility, and announce that this was an act of war.

Jontlwy: The world will be freaked.

Jontlwy: If it was indeed a particular country, we will go to war.

Jontlwy: But there's no way it was, directly, a country. I don't know how you respond to this.

Jontlwy: You can't just go running into Muslim countries looking for the guy.

Jontlwy: I really don't know.

Mikezly: How can they get all these planes hijacked? Where is the security?

Jontlwy: That's the big question.

Jontlwy: Something went terribly wrong.

Jontlwy: I think it might be 2 from Boston, 1 from DC, and 1 from NJ.

Jontlwy: I have no clue how security could let this go.

Jontlwy: People are going to have a major backlash against Muslims.

Mikezly: I still don't know how planes can just crash into buildings with such accuracy. I can't believe it to be that easy. The hijackers aren't pilots.

Jontlwy: It's not too hard. You see the building and run into it. But they got a bit "lucky" I guess that everything fell.

Jontlwy: No more world trade center. I can't believe it.

Jontlwy: The most heavily populated district in the U.S.

Mikezly: Not the pentagon. It's not a tall building.

Jontlwy: They didn't hit the pentagon with as much accuracy.

Mikezly: As I would imagine.

Jontlwy: People are going to be so angry.

Mikezly: It wasn't just one, it was an attack. Call it what u want, this is a war.

Mikezly: It doesn't have to be so obvious to call it a war.

Jontlwy: Oh yeah, it's a war.

Jontlwy: If they can find someone to declare war against, they will.

Mikezly: But it could take weeks or forever to find anything.

Jontlwy: True.

Mikezly: Answers don't just appear.

Mikezly: I believe that there won't be any answers.

Jontlwy: Mike, I have to end this conversation. Everyone is going home.

Mikezly: OK. Please speak to everyone and email with any word. I'll get online at 9 AM tomorrow to chat with anyone in the family.

Jontlwy: I'll let everyone know that's when you're getting online. I'll get online to chat with you and let you know of any new news. Stay put for now. Be safe and smart.

Mikezly: OK bro. Take care and be safe. I will speak to you tomorrow.

Mikezly: Love.

Jontlwy: Will do. Love.

Jontlwy: J out.

Mikezly: M out.

Mikezly: Peace.

Jontlwy: Peace.

I am sure very few people have a record of their experience on 9/11. I think the scariest part for me was that my first impressions of everything that happened came from my brother's brief descriptions. I hadn't seen a television yet, and the Internet wasn't showing anything substantial. How could anyone imagine a plane hitting the World Trade Center, and even more, the buildings falling down? It just doesn't make any sense. It never will.

Aside from trying to understand the actual events and evaluating my own safety, the majority of my conversation with my brother involved attempts to contact our family and friends to make sure they were safe. The following day, my entire family met online to discuss the tragic event and check in on how everyone was doing. My family had never gotten together online all at once to chat about anything ever before. Actually, most people in my family had never even used IM before. My priorities in life became clearer than ever. Nothing is more important than family and friends.

The September 11th disaster forced everyone to sit back and really think about what is important in their lives. 9/11 confirmed everything that I had time to reflect on during my trip. What I learned was that as long as you have your family and friends, you're going to be all right, no matter how much you struggle with day-to-day things. Life is too short to do things that don't make you happy. You never know what's going to happen, so you better do what you want to do now before it's too late. You don't get two shots at life (as far as we know), and this time around isn't a dry run. So, don't sit around on your couch and watch the tube all the time. Explore the world, sign up for a painting class, pick up an instrument, or write an article and send it to a newspaper. Do something that you always wanted to do but never seemed to find the time. Expanding our mind, and spirit, isn't something that should only be squeaked in after a long day of work. It's something that we must do continually if we are to live up to our potential as human beings.

AFTERMATH

CHAPTER 18

"There is only one success—to spend your life in your own way."

—Christopher Morley

Now that I'm back, I realize how important my trip was to my future and me. While 9/11 helped me put things in perspective with regard to the big picture, my trip helped me focus on things that I enjoy doing, rather than things that people think I should be doing. After the trip, I realized that I really enjoyed writing. Did that mean I would become a writer or a journalist? The answer is I really didn't know. I did know that I was going to continue to write, and I did know that I was going to work at a job where I could come home satisfied. It might sound so easy, that I should have been doing that in the first place, but for some reason it didn't seem that straightforward. Answers don't always stare you in the face. In the three years after I graduated from college, I managed to discover more about what I don't want to do in my life than what truly calls to me. But that can be important as well. It can also be frustrating, and can make someone who is otherwise motivated feel lost in our strange world. My time abroad allowed me to see the world and myself much more simply. All the debris that collected on me over time had clouded my perspective, but the baptism of my travels rinsed me clean. With fresh eyes, I saw things as I had never seen them before. My road ahead appeared less gravelly and dusty, at least for the time being.

A few weeks after I got back, my friend from Koh Tao came home from her trip and we caught up on all our travels and experiences. She talked to the principal at her school. He recommended that I substitute teach to see if I liked the classroom environment, and said if I was still interested he would definitely grant me an interview. After substituting for a few months, I knew I wanted to teach. I met with the principal, who gave me a full-time position for the next school year. It had to be the best break of my life, but I had earned it, and I felt I could do an excellent job. Would teaching be my calling? Time will only tell. As my parents preach, I just have to follow a course and see where it takes me. If it dead-ends, well, then you stop and turn around. But you need a plan and you must set goals. Otherwise, time will just pass you by.

I guess the only thing I regretted about my trip was that I left my diary on the plane during my trip home. I was reading over all my travels and stories on the plane, and simply forgot to put the journal in my bag. Desperately, I called the airline, but they said they didn't have it in their lost and found. I felt like a whole part of my trip was ripped away from me. Without the diary, I wouldn't have made it through all the ups and downs of my journey. Then, a month later, the telephone rang and a stranger was on the other line.

"Hi, I'm looking for Mike."

"Yeah, I'm him. If you're a telemarketer I'm not interested."

"No, no, no...I'm not a telemarketer. I'm not sure if this book I found is yours because it doesn't have a name on it, but I believe it's someone's diary. Whoever it belongs to left it behind on a plane. I had to read the whole thing to find a name in the book. Yours was the only full name I found in the entire journal. Unfortunately, your name is pretty common so I've called over ten people. Did you lose a journal?"

"You're kidding me. You found my diary? I can't believe you found my diary! I've been miserable over losing it. When did you find it? It's been over a month since I left it on the plane."

"Sorry for not calling earlier. I was on business traveling around, so I haven't been home in a while. There wasn't that much I could do about it."

"Don't worry about it. Is the book blue?"

"Yeah, its blue. It's your book. I live in San Francisco if you want to pick it up."

"That's great. I'll pick it up tomorrow if you don't mind."

"Not a problem. I can give you my address and just leave it in my mailbox."

"That's fine. Wait a minute, you said you read all my stories, right?"

"Yeah, like I said, there was no name throughout the entire book until near the end. I could tell it was very personal, so I felt bad reading your work. At the same time, I wanted to track down the owner, and that seemed to be the only logical way to find a name."

"I can't really say I'm happy about someone knowing all my stories and thoughts, but since you did read it, I guess I should ask you what you thought about my stories?"

"Like I said, I'm really sorry about doing that. I would never have read it without good reason. I do read many books in my job, though. That's why I was traveling. I was on a book tour with one of my authors. I'm a literary agent. We went all around Europe promoting his book. As for your writing, honestly, some of your stories are very funny. You've got some talent. You really seem to get inside a person's head. The comparison between sex and football was hilarious."

"You thought that was funny?"

"Are you kidding me, I was laughing out loud. All your stories were good. Some were funny while some had good points. Like the California Pizza Kitchen story."

"Wow. Thanks. I'm surprised."

"Well, look. You got talent, but talent isn't everything. If I was your agent, here's what I'd tell you. Put your stories together, do some serious editing, and when you're done, get back to me. I would love to read your stories when they're all cleaned up. And if it's good, which I think it can be, we'll see what we can do about publishing something. I'll put my business card inside the journal. How does that sound?"

"That's unbelievable! You never know what's going to happen, do you?"

"You've got that right, my friend."

0-595-24193-X

Printed in the United States
745800003B